For more than forty years,
Yearling has been the leading name
in classic and award-winning literature
for young readers.

Yearling books feature children's
favorite authors and characters,
providing dynamic stories of adventure,
humor, history, mystery, and fantasy.

Trust Yearling paperbacks to entertain,
inspire, and promote the love of reading
in all children.

Keep an eye out for Kristen Tracy's new book . . .

Camille McPhee Fell Under the Bus... by Kristen Tracy

A YEARLING BOOK

Copyright © 2009 by Kristen Tracy

All rights reserved. Published in the United States by Yearling,
an imprint of Random House Children's Books,
a division of Random House, Inc., New York.
Originally published in hardcover in the United States by Delacorte Press,
an imprint of Random House Children's Books,
a division of Random House, Inc., New York, in 2009.

Yearling and the jumping horse design
are registered trademarks of Random House, Inc.

Visit us on the Web! www.randomhouse.com/kids
Educators and librarians, for a variety of teaching tools, visit us at
www.randomhouse.com/teachers

The Library of Congress has cataloged the hardcover edition of this work as follows:
Tracy, Kristen.
Camille McPhee fell under the bus / Kristen Tracy.
p. cm.
Summary: Ten-year-old Camille McPhee relates the ups and downs of her
fourth-grade year at her Idaho elementary school as she tries to
adjust to the absence of her best friend, maintain control of her low
blood sugar, cope with the intensifying conflict between her parents,
and understand the importance of honesty and fairness.
ISBN 978-0-385-73687-9 (hardcover) — ISBN 978-0-385-90633-3 (lib. bdg.)
ISBN 978-0-375-89098-7 (e-book)
[1. Conduct of life—Fiction. 2. Schools—Fiction. 3. Friendship—Fiction.
4. Family problems—Fiction. 5. Idaho—Fiction.] I. Title.
PZ7.T68295Cam 2009
[Fic]—dc22
2008024903

ISBN 978-0-375-84546-8 (pbk.)

Printed in the United States of America

10 9 8 7 6 5 4 3 2 1

First Yearling Edition

FOR CARl jeAN tRACY—MY DAD!

Acknowledgments

This was the first book I ever wrote, and I'll try to thank all the people who helped me on my journey. First, thanks to Sara Crowe, who plucked Camille out of the slush pile and found her a great home. And lots of thanks to Wendy Loggia, who provided wonderful insight, advice, and smiley faces that helped make this book what it is today. I've come across a lot of good teachers in my life: Gail Wronsky, Leslie Norris, Brian Evenson, Kathryn Davis, Eric Zencey, Bonnie Ballif-Spanvill, David Rivard, and Stephen Dunn have been very encouraging folks. And I'd like to thank Al Young, who kindly pushed me in the direction of fiction, and Stuart Dybek, who read early adventures of Camille and thought I could do something more with them.

My family has been a source of both inspiration and encouragement for this book. I'd like to thank my sister, Julie Tracy Belnap, and her family for providing, among other things, the idea for the arthropod assignment. (Thanks, Rachel!) And thanks, Mom and Dad, for giving me such a strange and rural upbringing.

Friends looked at and discussed various versions of this book with me and provided useful feedback and support. Big thanks to Ulla Frederiksen, Jackie Srodes (and family!), Michelle Willis, Linda Young, Ellen Lesser, Sarah Lesser, Rick Zand, my friends at Sarducci's, Sarah Gessel Rich, Adam Schuitema, Joseph Legaspi, Stella Beratlis, and Scott Dykstra and the entire Dykstra clan.

And, of course, I must thank my elementary school bus driver, Linda Gilbert, for counting heads that fateful morning and realizing that a head was missing, because I'd fallen underneath her bus.

Fair: just, equitable, what is right.
Free of clouds or storms.

Unfair: the life of Camille McPhee.

CHAPTER 1

GETTING RUN OVER

When I woke up and kicked the covers off, I moved my legs back and forth in the air like superpowered scissors. I did this because I needed to get my blood moving. I needed to move my blood from my legs to my head so that when I stood up, I wouldn't get light-headed. My mom and dad thought that the reason I got light-headed was because I had low blood sugar. They said I was hypoglycemic.

You might think that someone with low blood sugar would be allowed to eat a lot of sugar. But I wasn't that lucky. When I felt shaky, I had to eat cheese. My parents said that I had to eat every three hours to keep my blood sugar levels stable. This meant that I had to carry extra food with me to school in a cooler.

I was the only student at Rocky Mountain Elementary School who was allowed to eat during class. I could open up my cooler and pull out a ham sandwich right at my desk whenever I wanted. And I did.

You might be thinking that I was a pretty fat fourth grader, but I wasn't. I weighed less than sixty pounds. Five of those pounds were from my hair. I was very lucky. I didn't have long, stringy hair like Polly Clausen or Gracie Clop. I had movie-star hair. It was thick, caramel brown, and beautiful.

When I walked outside on a sunny day, the sun bounced off my hair, making every strand shine like gold. It's a really good thing that I had great hair, because it helped camouflage my head. Some people thought it was big. And they enjoyed pointing this out. You might think that a big head of hair drew more attention to a big head.

Well, it did. But when people said some mean thing like "Hey, soccer-ball head," or "Why do you have a blimp attached to your neck?" or "What's up, hippo head?" (I always hated that one), then someone else pointed out that maybe it was just my hair making my head look big. And then the first person would argue that it wasn't my hair but my big goofy head that made my head look big.

There would always be a debate about this. No one was ever sure. Listening to people fight about whether or not I had a big head made me feel terrible. Once, it got so bad that I thought about cutting off all my hair and mailing it to my cousin Binna in Colorado. She had always been a huge fan of my hair at family reunions. But I didn't have to do that.

One day, like magic, a new teacher showed up at my school. Ms. Golden. She came from New Jersey. And one of the things she brought with her to Rocky Mountain Elementary School was very large and powerful hair. When she walked down the halls, her hair spilled off her in curls and waves. And because everybody liked Ms. Golden, big hair became very popular. And nobody teased me anymore.

I mean, nobody teased me about my big head anymore. You see, one winter day, right after I kicked my legs back and forth in the air like superpowered scissors, something really bad happened. It was a Friday, the day my mother taught a morning kickboxing class at the gym. She didn't leave to teach it until after I went to school, but she was a very dedicated instructor, and she always practiced her routine several times in the den. So I had to get ready by myself.

That Friday, I got up and put on fresh thermal

underwear. And jeans. And a fuzzy blue sweater that didn't itch me. Then I ate a bowl of cereal. And washed my face and brushed my teeth. And most important, like always, I fluffed my hair. For one whole minute. After that, I grabbed my books, pencils, chocolate-milk money, and cooler. I poked my head into the den and told my mother goodbye.

She appeared to be doing jumping jacks.

"See you when you get home," she said, panting.

When I went out to catch the bus, I thought it was going to be a great day. I walked down the front steps and blew a big cloud out into the cold February air in front of me. Then I took a deep breath. It was so cold that my lungs started to sting and my right nostril froze shut.

Of my two nostrils, it was usually the right one that froze shut. Because I was right-handed and my right arm was stronger than my left, I figured I was also right-nostriled. Which meant when I sucked in cold air, my right nostril sucked a lot harder than the left one, and that was why it would freeze shut.

But the awful thing that happened really doesn't have anything to do with my nostril.

I walked to the bus stop and stood in line behind Manny and Danny Hatten. They were identically mean twins and were in the sixth grade, which meant they were pretty tough. Nobody messed with those two, because Manny and Danny had muscles. Mostly in their legs. They were very good at kicking other people's backpacks and lunch boxes. And they were also very good at having greasy blond hair.

I lifted my right hand to my forehead to shade my eyes and look down the long, snowy road. In addition to the bus, I was also looking for my cat Checkers. I hadn't seen her for three years. But I still kept my eyes open just in case. I was what my mother called *hopeful*. I spotted my bus making its first stop at Coltman Road. It would be here in five minutes.

I lived on County Line Road. It was in the middle of nowhere. Across the street, there was a big hay field that stretched so far that it never stopped. During the winter, cows lived there. To keep them from escaping, a barbed-wire fence surrounded the field. And there was a steep drainage ditch that ran along the bottom of the field, next to the road. That was not a good place to wait for the bus. So we made our line on the side of the road with the driveways.

I checked my cooler to make sure that its lid was on tight; then I set it down in the snow. I didn't say anything to anyone. I wasn't much of a talker.

I mean, I used to be, but I wasn't anymore. After last September, when my very good friend, Sally Zook, moved to Japan with her family, I decided that I didn't need friends. So far, without Sally, fourth grade had been pretty rough.

I shifted my weight from my right boot to my left. Then I stood back and admired my snow-stamping job. I liked to leave tracks wherever I went. Doing that reminded me of an important fact that I learned about myself in second grade: I wasn't just a girl. I was also an animal. A mammal. If you are an animal with a backbone, and you aren't a mammal, you are either a fish or a bird or a reptile or an amphibian. But not an insect or a plant.

While admiring my stamping job, I heard a smacking sound. I looked up. Manny and Danny were throwing snowballs at Polly. The snowballs exploded on impact, breaking into countless icy pieces. One big clump got stuck in Polly's long, stringy hair.

"Stop it!" Polly yelled, taking off her backpack. She lifted it up in front of her and used it as a shield.

I was glad that they were throwing snow at Polly instead of me. It wasn't that they liked me or anything. The reason they threw snow at Polly and not me was because my father was a very big man with a very big temper.

Polly's father had been a skinny man who didn't have any temper. When we were in the first grade, he was killed in a car accident. His car slid on a patch of ice and another car slid on a patch of ice and the two cars mashed into each other. Everybody except Polly's dad lived.

"Don't expect life to be fair," my father said right after the accident. He was sitting at the kitchen table with the newspaper spread out in his lap. He pointed to a small square photo of Polly's dad. He bit into his doughnut and shook his head. "Don't expect life to be fair," he said again, folding up the paper and setting it aside.

I'm glad my dad told me that early on in life. Because until this happened, until Mr. Clausen slid on a stupid patch of ice, until he died and everyone else lived, I was expecting life to be pretty fair. In fact, I was expecting my own life to be terrific, lengthy, and at some point filled with ponies.

Polly got a couple more snowballs chucked at her, and I stood behind her with my head down. When trying to avoid making friends (and enemies), it's really important not to make eye contact with anyone, especially kids who are in your class.

I could hear the bus brakes gasping and squeaking. The bus lurched to a stop and we waited for Mrs. Spittle to wave for us to cross the road. She flashed the yellow lights and opened the door. When Mrs. Spittle opened the bus door, it always made the same sound, like somebody was letting out a breath.

Manny and Danny ran across the slick road, putting their weight in the heels of their cowboy boots, skidding most of the distance. They zoomed so fast that I worried they might end up in the drainage ditch. Polly had a weird way of walking. She did it with her pink boots angled out, like a duck waddling across the road on its floppy, webbed feet. Poor Polly. I walked like a normal fourth grader, one foot in front of the other. The only thing that wasn't normal was that in addition to my backpack, I also carried my small, bright blue cooler.

I lifted my cooler out of the snow and followed a few steps behind Polly. Friday was chocolate-milk day. I loved chocolate-milk day. It was the one day my mom didn't mind if I ate something sweet for lunch. I heard my chocolate-milk money jingle as I walked. I liked carrying money to school in my pocket. And I preferred change over bills. Because change jingled better. Anytime I had several quarters, I felt very rich, and I would do some extra shaking whenever I could.

Shake. Shake. Shake. Halfway across the road, there was a patch of black ice. Polly waddled across it just fine. But with my heavy backpack and cooler and jingling change, I was tripping over my own feet to catch my balance. The next thing I knew, the lid flew off my cooler, and my own banana hit me in the face. Then my butt and head smacked the frozen ground. And everything looked dark.

At first, I thought I had been knocked unconscious. People in my mother's soap operas were always being knocked unconscious. A lot of the time, they'd wake up with complete amnesia. But when I opened my eyes, I knew that it was chocolate-milk day and that I was Camille McPhee. And when I felt around me and grabbed my banana, I knew that I couldn't be unconscious, because an unconscious person wouldn't have been able to open her eyes and locate her banana so quickly.

Even with my eyes open, things were still pretty dark. I brushed my hair off my face and expected to see some light. But there wasn't any. That's when I realized that I was no longer underneath the bright Idaho sky. Somehow, I had fallen and slipped underneath Mrs. Spittle's bus. The underbelly of the bus was filthy. Dirty chunks of melting ice dripped onto me.

To the right and left of my head were big black tires. Snow was pressed deep into their treads. I groaned. Then I heard one of the worst sounds of my life. It was the one sound you never want to hear if you've slipped and fallen under your own school bus. I heard the sound of Mrs. Spittle shutting the bus door. *Sssspt*. Then, from somewhere deep in my own brain, I heard my father's words: "Don't expect life to be fair."

CHAPTER 2

DINGO STRATEGY

At that moment, I no longer worried about whether or not my life would be fair. I had a much scarier thought in my head. *If your school bus drives over you, does that mean you won't be alive anymore?* I rolled onto my stomach and pulled myself forward, out from beneath the bus. Once I cleared the bumper, I got onto my hands and knees. I crawled as fast as I could, faster than a cockroach trying to escape a shoe. I made it to the side of the road and tried to stand up. But instead,

I fell backward into a snowbank. Then I heard a good sound. Mrs. Spittle opened the bus door.

"Camille!" she yelled. "Are you okay?"

I was flat on my back, staring up into the sun. Mrs. Spittle got out of her bus and helped me stand up.

"I didn't even see you, Camille. Are you all right?" Mrs. Spittle brushed the snow off my coat with energetic swats. It felt a little bit like she was karate-chopping me with her bare, big-knuckled hands.

I nodded. Mrs. Spittle grabbed my backpack and cooler and handed them to me.

"An all-white coat is a bad idea," she said. She put her hands on her hips and looked down at me. "You even have on white boots. That outfit is a complete safety hazard. You blend in with the scenery."

I stretched my arms out and looked at my coat. It was no longer pure white. Dirty slush and ice had spattered dark spots all down my front. I looked like a Dalmatian.

"Are you good enough to board and go to school?" she asked.

I looked at the steps leading up to the bus.

"We ran over Camille McPhee!" somebody shouted from inside. Multiple gasps floated out of the bus's open door.

Mrs. Spittle charged back onto her bus.

"Nobody ran over anybody!" she yelled down the aisle. She swung her blond bob ferociously from side to side.

"I think I see blood," Danny said. "I think we cracked her head open."

Mrs. Spittle pulled the bus's handset from the loudspeaker.

"Listen up," she said. "Camille is fine. She did not receive any open wounds."

"I can see blood all over her coat!" somebody said.

Mrs. Spittle placed her hand out in front of her, as if she were signaling them to stop. "There is no blood. Camille's coat has been splattered with dirty snow. She fell down. She fell under the bus."

I heard everybody on the bus laughing hard. I felt more and more light-headed. I wondered how long it would take everyone to forget about Camille McPhee falling under a school bus. I hoped two weeks.

"The next person who makes a sound is getting a written warning," Mrs. Spittle said into the handset. She talked so loudly that the loudspeaker squeaked, releasing sounds like metal scraping metal. "And the person after that is going to get a written warning *and* help me clean up this bus."

She had silenced everyone. Written warnings got mailed to your parents. And cleaning up the bus meant coming face to face with dangerous floor garbage. She looked at me.

"Camille, are you going to board?" she asked, sitting back down in the driver's seat.

I looked into my cooler. Everything had fallen out, even my orange. I was already feeling shaky, and I could see my ham sandwich and mozzarella sticks lying lifeless in their plastic Baggies underneath the bus. Then I looked back up the stairs. The metal ridges designed to prevent slipping were coated in slush. I turned and looked at the long row of blurry faces fogging the windows, staring out at me. The bus looked full. Who would I sit next to? Usually, I didn't care. But today I did.

"I don't feel good," I said, tears rolling onto my cheeks.

"You're not coming to school?" Mrs. Spittle asked, fastening her seat belt.

I shook my head.

She frowned. "From now on, please walk slowly. It's your best and safest rate of speed."

"Okay," I said.

I crept back across the road, this time waddling like Polly, and waited at the top of my driveway. Once the bus left, I wanted to pick up my food. Mrs. Spittle waved to me as the bus leapt forward and rolled down the road. I waved back, and as I did, one of the bus's back tires ran over my orange, squashing it flat, shooting juice and pulp several feet. One large squirt landed right in my eye.

After some rubbing, I opened my eyes and saw Mr. Lively's dog, Pinky, dart into the road for my sandwich. I had two neighbors: the Livelys and the Bratbergs. I thought they were both interesting. But only one of them had a dog. Pinky was a pure white and deaf Dalmatian. My dad called him an albino. Mr. Lively was a very thin and mostly hairless person who only heard you when you yelled his name really loud several times. I watched Pinky inhale my sandwich and scarf down all my food. I hoped he hadn't eaten the wrappers. Those aren't good for dogs.

"Camille! Camille!"

The sound was coming from the Bratbergs'. I looked into their yard. I didn't see anybody.

"Up here!"

I looked up. Four people were standing on top of the house: Mrs. Bratberg and her three kids—Dustin, Brody, and Samantha. Those three used to ride the bus with me. But not anymore. They got kicked off. And it's permanent. Because they opened up the back emergency door while we were moving and threw a first grader's backpack out onto the road. And it had a Game Boy in it.

I felt some sympathy for them, because they didn't know that the backpack had a Game Boy in it. Because backpacks aren't made out of see-through material. After that, the Bratbergs didn't go to school. They learned everything at home.

"Camille! Are you sick?" Mrs. Bratberg called to me.

"Not really," I said. "Are you stuck on your house?"

"No, I'm teaching a lesson about gravity."

I watched her drop something off the roof. It looked like a wad of tinfoil. All the Bratbergs stared at it.

"What was that?" I asked.

"Leftovers," Mrs. Bratberg said.

It was clear to me that learning science in school was nothing like learning science at home.

"Is your father in town?" she asked.

I shook my head. I did not think it was smart to yell the answer, because a robber might have heard me.

"Can you come over and be a mother's helper tomorrow?" she asked.

"Yes," I said.

Mrs. Bratberg ran a business in her house, and sometimes she needed an extra set of hands to watch her kids. She sold things on eBay. Mostly it was stuff from her basement and garage that looked old. For a while, I thought they were antiques. But Mrs. Bratberg called them retro bargains. She said they were things from her childhood, like records and lamps and hot pants, that had become valuable again. I could only be a mother's helper when my father was out of town. He didn't want me to watch the Bratberg kids even if their mom was in the next room. Because he thought I was too young to handle dangerous situations. And he thought the Bratbergs were very dangerous.

Mrs. Bratberg waved to me.

"I only need you for an hour," she said.

I waved back. That was a relief. The Bratbergs sucked a lot of my energy. I watched her throw something else off their roof. It looked like a loaf of bread. Then I turned to go inside. When I climbed the front steps to my house, my legs wobbled like pudding.

I kicked off my snow boots at the front door and stumbled down the hall in my socks. I felt very dizzy. I didn't peek back in at my mother. I wasn't ready to talk about my day yet. When I got to my room, I collapsed on my squeaky bed. I crawled under the covers and tried to pretend like none of this had happened. Like fourth grade was still going pretty good.

Did you just fall underneath Mrs. Spittle's bus? Did you just miss chocolate-milk day? Did Pinky just eat all your food and is your blood sugar so low that you could slip into a coma? I groaned and reached for some jelly beans that I kept in my dresser drawer. Because I didn't have a single friend who would stick up for me, I was sure everybody at school was laughing about what had

16

happened. I was sure that nobody cared about how I was doing, or if I'd suffered a contusion.

I'd suffered one of those before. The summer before second grade, I fell off the diving board at the public swimming pool the wrong way. Instead of falling forward, into the water, I fell sideways, onto the cement. It's actually very easy to do. Because those boards are quite wet and bouncy. And the swimming instructors make you jump off them in your bare, slippery feet.

Sally was in my swim class, and after I fell that day she came and found me in the locker room and told me, "Diving is very dangerous. They should put pillows around the pool edges." I held a bag of frozen peas to my head and agreed with her. But nobody in my school was as nice as Sally. They were all a bunch of laughers. I hoped Japan understood how lucky it was to have her.

I wiped some hot tears off my cheeks and tried not to think so much about Sally Zook. But it was hard. Sally was very important to me. I'd wanted to be her friend from the moment I met her in her purple swimsuit. Because Sally looked a lot like Snow White, and I thought that was neat. She had pale skin, dark hair, and blue eyes, and even though she was allergic to coconut, that's exactly what she smelled like. After we became friends in swim class, all through second and third grades she saved me a seat on the bus. Sometimes our mothers took us to the mall.

We did all the things very good friends do. Except we didn't e-mail each other. Because her parents were afraid of computers. They had one. But Sally wasn't allowed to use it. Except for playing video games about math and spelling. And neither one of us liked those games. We liked playing real games together. Like who could run the fastest with an egg on a spoon. Or who could hold an ice cube the longest. Or who could throw my mother's couch cushions the farthest. But then everything changed. Sally's dad took a job in Japan.

At first, I wasn't worried, because Manny and Danny told Sally that it was against the law to move to a country that we'd fought against in a war. But they were wrong. When the Zooks moved in September, I sat on my front steps with my mom and we watched Sally leave. Sally waved to me from the back window of her car as her family drove to the airport, and even though I tried not to, I cried. Before she left, she promised to write and send me a bathrobe. (She called it a kimono, but the way she described it made it sound exactly like a bathrobe.) I never heard from her again.

Because, like my mother said, I was *hopeful*, I thought that when I made a friend I would have that friend in my life forever. But Sally only lasted two years. For the rest of September, I moped around the house. I moped so much that my parents took me to the zoo. There was a touring exhibit of a pack of dingoes.

As I stood watching all these dingoes, I noticed one dingo off by itself in the corner. It looked shinier than the other dingoes. Maybe that was because it was the only dingo in the sun.

As I watched that shiny dingo, I realized that it didn't care about the rest of the pack. It looked totally content. It looked proud. And happy. I also noticed that it had a stubby tail, one only half as long as the other dingoes' tails. If I were a dingo, that would have really bugged me, and I probably would have tried to lie on my tail so no one else could see how wimpy it looked. But this dingo didn't care a fig about the other feisty, nipping, bushy-tailed dingoes.

That was when some guy in the crowd said, "Look at that smart dingo in the corner, flying under the radar."

The man was talking about my dingo. That was when I realized that without Sally, the rest of fourth grade was going to be really rough. Because I didn't need friends who would leave me or forget important promises. I needed to find myself a corner where I could sit and admire myself. So I hatched a plan. From that point on, at school, I was going to try to fly under the radar too. Other than falling underneath my own bus, I thought I was doing a decent job so far.

I ate some more jelly beans and waited for my mother to finish practicing her routine. I knew she wouldn't be mad at me. My mother was very sympathetic to people who fell down. Once, when she was my age, she had fallen down an escalator. She called it her only near-death experience. At department stores, she still took her time getting on escalators.

The jelly beans helped. I felt much less fuzzy. I was about to drift into a wonderful sleep. But I didn't. I never realized how loud our phone was until it started to ring. My mother didn't answer it. From my bedroom I heard the machine pick up. And it was a voice I recognized. It was Jimmy! The guy who worked at the paint counter at Home Depot. Jimmy was also a contractor. My mother had hired him to do some construction work for us—without my father's permission. Which meant, of course, big trouble.

CHAPTER 3

lies

"Maxine," Jimmy said. "I can knock that wall out today!"

When I heard this, my stomach began feeling awful, like I'd just eaten eggplant. (Eggplant is a risky vegetable for me.) Jimmy's news was terrible. Why? Knocking down walls was all part of the crisis.

The crisis started when my mother stopped watching soap operas and became a certified aerobics instructor. Her specialty was kickboxing. This meant that she chopped and kicked the air in front of her on a pretty regular basis. Mostly, this happened in the den or the kitchen. She'd plant her feet and yell, "Hook! Uppercut! Hook! Uppercut!" She liked to throw her punches in the direction of the refrigerator.

When she agreed to teach an early-morning class at a nearby gym, she told me that she might not be able to spend as much "quality time" with me as she normally did before school. But she'd pack my cooler for me at night. And nothing else would change. That's when my father explained what was really happening here. My mother had turned forty and she was having a midlife crisis. He said that I shouldn't take anything she did personally. He said that was how *he* was going to handle it.

But her midlife crisis was not a small thing. Even though my father said that we couldn't afford it because we'd just gotten out of the hole, my mother wanted to change everything: the color of the walls, the carpet, the furniture, the roof, the kitchen appliances. She even wanted to replace the toilet seat.

"Imagine how much better it would feel with a little cushion on it," she told my father.

"I don't want to imagine it with a little cushion, Maxine. We don't need it. We need to stay out of the hole."

These were the last words my father spoke before he left on a business trip to Seattle.

I heard my mother turn off her music. My coat made me sweat, but I didn't feel like taking it off. Underneath my hood, my hair felt like somebody had warmed it in an oven. I cocked my head so I could see out my bedroom door. A bright pink blur flew down the hall. Then the bright pink blur zoomed back in the other direction. She replayed Jimmy's message.

"Mother," I groaned.

She didn't come.

"Mother," I groaned again.

She popped her head in my bedroom.

"Did you miss the bus?" she asked.

When she said the word *bus,* I couldn't help myself. I started to cry.

"Are you sick?" she asked, taking a few steps into my room.

When she asked me this, it made me realize that I'd eaten way too many jelly beans. I felt like I could throw up. But I held it back.

"I think I am," I said, lifting my head up off the pillow. I had decided not to tell my mother about the bus. It was too embarrassing. Being hit by a bus was one thing, but falling underneath it was a totally different story.

"How come you're wearing your coat?" she asked.

That was a good question.

"I tried to go to school, but it didn't work," I said.

My mother came and sat at the foot of my bed. She pressed her hand against my forehead.

"You're burning up," she said. She unzipped my coat and peeled me out of it. "Wow. These mud spots are huge."

I nodded. "Yes. They are."

"Did you drop your coat in a puddle?" she asked.

"No," I said. And this wasn't a lie. Because when I was underneath the bus, I wasn't anywhere near a puddle. I landed on top of ice and snow and the road and maybe one of my mozzarella sticks.

She turned my coat over.

"They're everywhere!" she said. "I'm going to have to wash it at least twice. Maybe three times. Plus, I'll have to soak it."

"The world is a dirty place," I said. Then I changed the subject. "I still feel hot."

She touched my forehead again.

"You're very warm," she said, frowning. "Schools are little plague factories. You might have caught something. Don't worry. I'll call the attendance office and square away your absence."

"Okay," I said. "But I probably don't need my homework. Today was mostly math and PE and social studies and science and other things that I don't mind missing until Monday."

My mother frowned. "I'm going to get your homework, Camille."

Before I could argue against this idea, she looked at her watch and jumped to her feet.

"I need to get a substitute for my class," she said.

"Really?" I asked.

This was the first time this had ever happened. It felt very dramatic.

"What choice do I have?" She kissed my forehead. "You smell like an orange, Camille." She tilted her head and smiled. Then the bright pink blur ran from my room.

It was not fun being in bed. I wasn't *really* sick. I didn't have a good book to read. I was tired of eating jelly beans. I wanted chocolate milk. And having a cat with me would have been nice. Cats are great company. They lick. They purr. I loved cats. Sadly, my last three—Checkers, Fluff, and Muffin—were no longer with me. I was a very unlucky cat owner. After Checkers vanished, Fluff used up his ninth life falling out of a very tall tree, and Muffin was hit by a mail truck, both of my parents banned cats.

When we buried Muffin in the field behind our house, my father made a cross out of two Popsicle sticks. He wrote Muffin's name on it and stuck it in the ground.

"You're the kind of person who should own fish," he said.

My mother walked back into my room. She looked sad.

"I couldn't find a substitute. The gym canceled my class," she said.

"Forever?" I asked.

She shook her head. "Just today."

"I could stay by myself," I said.

"No," my mother said. "I'm not leaving my sick child home alone."

I thought that was probably the right decision. Even though I didn't enjoy hearing her call me a child. Because in a year, I would turn eleven. So I basically considered myself a "young person." I watched my mother mope out of my room. Then I closed my eyes. I guess I must have snoozed. Because the next time I saw her, she was showered and dressed and looked pretty fantastic. She was even smiling! This made me happy, because it meant canceling her kickboxing class wasn't the worst thing that had ever happened to her.

"I have some great news," she said. Tiny silver dolphins attached to her charm bracelet swam in the air around her wrist.

"I don't have any homework?" I asked.

She shook her head. "No, that I'm picking up this afternoon." She sat down next to me and stroked my hair. "Camille, here's something I've been thinking about concerning the idea of telling the whole truth."

"Uh-oh," I said. Because I knew that sometimes my mother was a fibber.

"Camille, sometimes telling the whole truth can

hurt people we love. Sometimes the whole truth can be so alarming that if we told the people we loved the whole truth, they wouldn't love us anymore."

After saying this, my mother frowned. So did I. Because it seemed like the polite thing to do. But then her frown somehow snapped into a smile.

"I've decided to move forward with some essential home repairs." Her eyes began to sparkle. "Your father would not be happy about this. Let's face it. We both love him, but he isn't always reasonable."

I nodded. I thought she would talk about all the ways we didn't find my father reasonable. He watched too much football. He had a difficult time being nice to our mail carrier. He used too much ketchup on his hash browns. He wouldn't let me be a mother's helper for the Bratbergs. And he refused to eat brownies if they didn't have walnuts in them.

"Your father doesn't understand how important it is to make essential home repairs. Therefore, because we both love your father, we're not going to tell him." She brushed a curl from her face and smiled at me.

I pulled my hand out from under the covers and pointed my finger at her. "I don't want to lie."

My mother sat down next to me and wrapped her hand around my finger. The tiny dolphins bounced against me, poking my skin with their sharp little snouts.

"Just because you're not telling the whole truth to someone doesn't mean that you're lying." She blinked at me several times, trying to look innocent.

"That's exactly what it means to tell a lie!" I said. I pulled my finger out of her hand and reaimed it at her.

The doorbell rang. It was Jimmy. Before leaving my room, my mother looked back at me over her shoulder. "You don't have to lie. But you don't have to tell him either." She blew me a kiss, but her aim was off. I think it landed on the floor.

CHAPTER 4

SAVING the WALL

I was really surprised in first grade when I heard the story about George Washington cutting down the cherry tree. After he chopped it down, his father asked him, "Who cut down this cherry tree?" And George Washington didn't lie. George Washington told his father, "I cut down that cherry tree."

But I was even more surprised in second grade, when I learned that this story was made up. George Washington never said those words. Also, he didn't have fake wooden teeth. His dentures were made of cows' teeth, human teeth, and elephant tusks.

Anyway, because my mother had a habit of not telling the truth, and because she'd taught me this same habit, and because George Washington's story wasn't even true, I thought everybody told some lies. I didn't understand that lying was such a bad thing. As long as I wasn't lying to a police officer or a 911 operator, as long as I told lies that didn't really matter (like being a mother's helper for the Bratbergs), I thought it was okay.

"Camille, I thought you'd be in school," Jimmy said. He set down a big saw on the living room carpet. "Look at your hair. It's so fluffy." As he talked, he reached toward my head, and I ducked.

When your hair has a lot of volume, this happens quite a bit. Either people love it and want to put their hands all over it. Or they make fun of you and try to shoot spit wads in it. Reactions differ depending on how they feel about big hair.

"Camille is sick today," my mother said.

Actually, due to the day's events, that lie was becoming more and more true.

I followed Jimmy and my mother to the kitchen table. Masking tape, paintbrushes, and sheets of plastic were crowded on one corner. That's when I noticed the pencil marks. The wall that separated the kitchen from the living room had big squares, almost the size of windows, penciled all over it. My mouth dropped open.

"You can't saw down that wall," I said.

"I didn't want to saw it down," my mother said. "I wanted to cut a big hole in it to open up the space. But it turns out, after consulting with Jimmy, that it's easier to just get rid of it."

My mother walked in front of the wall and knocked on it.

"Do you hear that, Camille? I'm all boxed in." She kept thumping on the wall with her fists. "This kitchen is too small. It's like a cage."

"No, it's not," I said.

"Yes, it is. And I'm a bird!" she yelled. "And I'm trapped."

My mother began to flap her arms, pretending they were wings. She flapped them very hard and ran into the living room.

"But once the wall comes down, I'll be free!" she yelled.

"You're a mammal, not a bird," I said.

But she didn't hear me. She began to punch and kick the air. This made no sense. I'd never seen a bird that could kickbox.

This was very, very bad. I looked at Jimmy. And his saw. I couldn't let it happen. Before I even knew what I

31

was doing, I was standing on top of the kitchen table and protesting.

"I love that wall. And my father loves that wall." I balled one hand up into a fist and pumped it over my head. "You'll have to saw through me to knock it down." I jumped into the air and yelled, "Save the wall!"

"Camille McPhee, get off the table," my mother said.

But I didn't get down, even though I felt very alone up there. I jumped and yelled again.

This time when I went up, my head hit the kitchen chandelier. And this time when I came down, my foot landed on a roll of masking tape. I shuffled my feet to catch my balance, but somehow I wound up on the sheets of plastic.

Both my mother's and Jimmy's mouths looked like perfect Os, full of surprise, as I toppled off the table and crashed to the floor. Ouch.

My mother hooked her hands under my armpits to lift me up. As she brought me to my feet, her biceps grew round and hard, like stones.

"Eventually, your father will forget the wall was ever there," she said.

This made no sense to me. Walls were big. And this one was an important part of our house. How could a person think another person would forget a wall?

"No, he won't," I said.

"Sure he will," she said.

"He will not!" I said. And a little bit of spit flew out of my mouth and hit Jimmy on the chin. It was rare that I got this foaming mad.

"Oh, Camille," Jimmy said, ignoring my spit mark, "sooner or later, we forget most things. It's part of being human."

This scared me a little bit. Because in addition to being a mammal, I was also a human. So this meant they were talking about me, too. I looked at my mother. She folded her arms across her chest.

"He's right. It takes about a year," she said. "A person can adjust to anything in a year."

"There have been studies," Jimmy said.

And rather than argue, I sort of believed them. Because I was always hearing about important studies on CNN. Plus, I started thinking about stuff from a year ago, and I couldn't remember all sorts of things. Like what flavor toothpaste I liked best at the time. Or important facts about Jupiter that I'd been taught in science. Or how I felt about pineapple served with cottage cheese. I'd had some the week before and I really liked it, but how had I felt about that combination a year ago? I couldn't remember.

That's when I was hit by a supersad thought. Sally was already starting to forget me, because she hadn't written. Or sent me my kimono. She'd been gone six months—half a year. As unfair as this sounded, it meant that I was halfway forgotten. "A year?" I asked.

Both Jimmy and my mother nodded. I looked at the doomed wall. It held all three of our shadows. I waved goodbye to it. And my shadow waved back.

"My mind is made up," my mother said. "The wall is history."

But something inside of me could not accept this. Because when I looked at that wall, I thought of something. We had taken a bunch of pictures in front of this wall. And we had saved them in my scrapbook. And even if my dad did forget about the wall, he'd remember it all over again when he saw those pictures. The only solution would be to burn my scrapbook. And I liked my scrapbook. So that meant I had to save the wall. "Save the wall!" I yelled again, jumping to my feet. My head felt very fuzzy, but that didn't stop me. I grabbed Jimmy's electric saw and darted outside. It was freezing, and I didn't have on my coat, but sometimes being a rebel means that you have to suffer.

If my father came back from Seattle and that wall was gone, he would freak out. All year long. It would be so awful that a blood vessel might pop in his brain. Or maybe he'd have a heart attack. And if something happened to him, even though I'm human, I didn't think I'd be able to forget about him in a year.

No. I could tell by how sad Polly looked standing in the bus line that she hadn't forgotten her father. She looked like she wished he was still around. But that's not how life works. After somebody dies, that person doesn't get to be around anymore. Ever.

CHAPTER 5

PURPLED

After I ran outside, I wasn't sure what to do. So I threw the saw into a snowbank. Then I covered it with a bunch more snow. And the broken bough of a pine tree. And even more snow. I hadn't realized this about myself, but I was pretty good at hiding power tools. I ran back inside and slammed the door so fast that my movie-star hair slapped me right in the face. A clump of it swung into my mouth and got stuck there and I spit it out. Then I presented my two empty hands. I thought taking the saw would slow my mother down. But I should have known better.

"Camille, it doesn't matter if you hide Jimmy's saw. The world is big. There'll always be another saw."

My mother walked outside. When she came back, she was holding the saw and shaking the slush off it. I guess I wasn't as good at hiding power tools as I thought. She set the saw down and frowned at me. That's when Jimmy pulled out a tool called a stud finder. He placed it flat against the wall and dragged it across the surface. Then he grunted.

"That doesn't sound good," my mother said.

"Maxine, I'm having second thoughts about this wall," he said.

I rubbed my hands together. I hoped Jimmy's second thoughts about the wall were a lot like my first thoughts.

"My vision is changing," he said.

My mother gasped.

"Well, if you're losing your vision, maybe you should see an eye doctor," I said. "And stay away from our wall," I added.

"The cost," he said. "The damage. Why don't you paint it your favorite color and turn it into a meditation wall?"

My mother didn't look too thrilled. But I did. I

was starting to like Jimmy a lot more than I had five minutes earlier.

A meditation wall didn't sound bad at all. I smiled. I felt that with Jimmy's help, I'd saved what I needed to save.

Because my mother didn't want to leave me home alone, Jimmy went to the store and brought back her number-one paint choice. I didn't ask what color it was. I wanted to wake up in the morning and be surprised. After a dinner of chicken noodle soup and wheat crackers, I went to bed. In my dreams, I could hear the swish of a paint roller.

That night, I dreamed about Sally. She rode a purple bicycle all over Japan without me. She steered dangerously close to the ocean, but she never fell in. I kept yelling her name, but she couldn't hear me, because I was living in Idaho. Then she stopped her bike and yelled at a low-flying bird, "Why don't you call me, Camille? Seriously. I know you've been banned from making long-distance calls, but why don't you buy an international calling card or something!"

When I woke up, I was surprised that a fourth grader could have such a meaningful dream. Or that Sally knew I'd been banned from making long-distance calls. Or that she would yell at a bird like that. But she did. Suddenly, I knew what I needed to do to make Sally stop forgetting me. I needed to call her. Also, I could remind her to send me that kimono. Because maybe she'd forgotten what size I was.

Figuring this out made starting my day feel very good. Because I had a plan. I would dig through our sofa cushions and look for loose change. And after that, I would babysit the Bratbergs. And maybe I'd even ask to be paid in quarters, so I could jingle and feel rich all the way home. I left my room that morning anxious to see what color my mom had painted the meditation wall.

Uh-oh. I walked through the house with my mouth wide open. I couldn't believe it. For some reason, in addition to the meditation wall, my mom had decided to paint every inch of our house purple. Even the baseboards and the light switches. Wow. This wasn't good. I knew my father would explode. But there wasn't much I could do about that now. So I ate a banana and decided to get to work.

A sofa can be very deep. I reached in all the way up to my shoulder. I looked underneath it with a flashlight, too. But I only found ninety cents. And a dirty sock. And a receipt from Taco Bell. But I also found something that made me sad: a toy mouse. I wasn't sure which cat it had belonged to, but since Muffin and Fluff were buried in my backyard, I decided to believe it was Checkers's toy mouse. I also decided to go outside and try to find Checkers again. Because when it came to finding her, I didn't think there was anything wrong with being *hopeful*.

My mother didn't even notice me leaving. I went outside in my coat and walked around to the backyard. I didn't call out to Checkers, because even when I owned her, she'd never come to me when I did that. I tried to sneak up on places where I thought she might hide. Like bushes. And snowdrifts. And Mr. Lively's woodpile. I figured that after living on her own for this long, she had probably become a very wild cat. Because Checkers had to make it on her own out here. And this was a wild place. There was a lot of dangerous stuff like cars. And raccoons. And spiders. And blizzards. And rusty nails. Also, there was no cat food.

"What are you looking for, Camille?"

I couldn't believe it. It was Polly. And she was wearing really cute jeans and a puffy green coat and pretty pink boots and standing right on my property.

"Nothing," I said.

Because what I was doing was none of her business. And if I'd told her the truth, that I was looking for my cat, she might have thought that I was too poor to afford a new cat. And that was not the problem. The problem was that sometimes I was an unlucky mammal who happened to own other unlucky mammals as pets.

"Are you feeling okay?" Polly asked.

"Of course," I said.

"That's good. It was very slippery out yesterday," Polly said.

I didn't say anything. I thought it was pretty rude to bring that up. Because I hadn't been thinking about falling underneath my school bus in front of all those laughers. I'd been thinking about something important. My poor cat Checkers.

"Do you want to build a snow fort?" Polly asked.

I did not say anything. I walked away. Because I was not in the mood to deal with Polly Clausen. If I was really going to be a dingo, I needed to learn how to walk away from a lot of people. And, if I came across them, other dingoes. I marched right over to a back corner of my yard and sat down and began admiring myself. Polly watched me for a little bit, but then she turned around and walked across Mr. Lively's yard back to her own property. Which was the right thing to do. Because coming over to my house wearing her cute jeans and puffy green coat and pretty pink boots and asking me to build a snow fort with her was the sort of thing that would wreck my dingo strategy.

Because dingoes didn't care about people or fashion. Dingoes went around naked. And dingoes didn't build snow forts, either. It was like Polly didn't even know what a dingo was or something. So I sat there in the corner until my butt got cold. Then I went inside to pack my cooler so I could help out Mrs. Bratberg.

Flat on her back in the living room, my mother stared up at the purple ceiling.

"Isn't it fabulous?" she asked.

"It is very noticeable," I said.

"Yeah. It really pops," she said.

And I thought that was a good word to use, because I knew that my dad's head was going to pop right off when he got back from Seattle and saw our purple house.

"I'm going to be a mother's helper for the Bratbergs," I said.

"Good luck," my mother said. "And let's not tell your father."

"I know," I said.

"Do you have your cooler?" she asked.

"Yes," I said.

"And don't let them put their turtle in the refrigerator this time. That's cruel," my mother said.

"I know. I won't."

Last time, they'd stuck that fellow in the crisper drawer to play a trick on me. I went in there looking for carrots. It was not a pleasant surprise.

"Camille," she said. Her voice sounded goofy. "I need to tell you something."

"Okay," I said.

"I bought something," she said.

"Is it a goat?" I asked.

42

Because I'd always secretly hoped to be a goat owner. "Better," she said.

But I couldn't think of anything better than a goat. So I didn't guess again.

"Carpet!" She rolled over onto her stomach and slapped the floor. "For your room, too. They're laying it first thing Monday. Finally, the whole house will match."

I was both happy and sad. I was happy because my mother was excited. But I was sad because I knew that my father was going to see all this new stuff and be so worried about going back in the hole that he'd blow up. It would have been a different story if she'd won the new carpet. But she hadn't.

While blowing up, my dad loved to yell, "Don't try to manipulate me, Maxine."

And my mother's favorite line to yell back was "If you wanted a tightwad, you should've married a tightwad."

Before Sally moved, I spent the night at her house a few times and her parents never yelled at each other. They played chess. We didn't have that game. We had Monopoly and Sorry and Twister and Battleship. And I have found that those games encourage yelling. (And cheating.)

As I walked over to the Bratbergs', it was nice to get away from all those paint fumes. While helping Mrs.

Bratberg, I always stayed very alert, and I never acted like a dingo. That would've been a mistake. I took a deep breath and rang their doorbell. Mrs. Bratberg opened the door and then smacked her forehead with the heel of her hand.

"Camille, I forgot to call you. We don't need you today. My mother's here. She's going to help me."

"Okay," I said.

"Here's a quarter for coming over," she said. "I'm sorry."

I took her quarter. She shut the door. Then I picked up a little rock so I could put it in my pocket and make my quarter jingle. It was not my favorite way to jingle, but it worked. Walking home, I heard a ton of screaming coming from the Bratbergs' house.

"Do not put your underwear in the microwave!"

"You cannot use glue in that manner!"

"Get your grandma out of that plastic bag!"

I guess I was happy that I wasn't at the Bratbergs'. I felt tired. I probably didn't have the energy needed to properly look after those three. Walking home, jingling my rock and quarter, I thought about where I might find more loose change. Maybe inside the clothes hamper. Or in my parents' pants pockets.

Shake. Shake. Shake. On the outside, my house looked very normal. But I knew that wasn't the truth. I knew that last night my mother had purpled our house. As I pulled open the back door and saw those walls again, I hoped that maybe secretly my dad loved the color purple. Maybe the reason he never wore purple or mentioned purple or bought anything purple wasn't related to the fact that he probably hated purple. Maybe he'd step inside our house and yell, "I love this, Maxine! Who cares about whether or not we're back in the hole. Let's buy a pizza and celebrate!"

CHAPTER 6

HOMEWORK BLUES

Sunday, after lunch, my mother set my schoolbooks and a stack of papers down in front of me. I blinked at them several times.

"It should only take an hour," she said, patting me on the head.

"If I can do all my homework in an hour at the kitchen table, why do I have to spend all day at school?" I asked.

And for a second, I thought maybe I could convince

my mother to let me miss school for a few months and sit and learn at the kitchen table instead.

"Camille, you're not going to drop out of the fourth grade," my mother said. "Life has ups. And life has downs." She traced her pointer finger through the air like it was climbing a series of mountains. Then I watched her finger drop to her side.

"Okay," I said.

"Do you want a piece of cheese?" she asked.

My mother thought cheese was good for me because it had protein in it. And protein was supposed to be good for keeping blood sugar levels stable.

I nodded. Then I opened up my social studies book. I didn't read the chapter first. I skipped to the end of it and read the questions to see what I was expected to learn. My mother handed me a mozzarella stick.

"What's your chapter about?" she asked.

"Laws," I said.

My mother wrinkled her forehead.

"For social studies? Last we talked you were making a map of the Oregon Trail," she said.

"That was October," I said. "I don't even have that map anymore. It got recycled."

"Wow," my mom said, wrinkling her forehead even more. "I've been so buried in learning my aerobics routines that I haven't kept up with your curriculum."

I had never heard my mother use the word *curriculum* before, but I agreed that she'd been buried in aerobics.

"What are you learning about laws?" she asked.

"I'm supposed to explain their benefits," I said.

"Really?" my mother asked. "In fourth grade? That sounds advanced."

And for one second, I got very excited, because I thought maybe I could convince my mother to let me learn at the kitchen table after all.

"Yes," I said. "Mr. Hawk is very advanced. He used to teach sixth grade. It's all he knows. This is his first year teaching fourth grade. Last month, for social studies, we studied the Vikings, and I had to know about their activities and personalities. Plus, I also had to learn about the Viking warriors, and that meant reading about their armor, weapons, and battle strategies."

My mother's eyes were very big.

"Are all your subjects this advanced?" she asked.

I nodded with a lot of enthusiasm.

"I should have done a better job staying on top of this," she said.

"The other day, in math, Mr. Hawk said that we were going to study bar graphs and charts. And for science, we have to identify 'local environmental issues' and possibly conduct scientific tests. *Possibly*," I said.

"I don't believe it," my mother said. "That doesn't sound fair."

"It's not! It's not! And science is where Mr. Hawk is the most advanced," I said. "Sometimes he uses words like *nucleus* and *organism* and *metric*."

"Camille, what you're telling me is very serious. I think I'm going to need to talk to your teacher about it."

She sat down next to me and rubbed my arm. Hearing that my mother wanted to talk to Mr. Hawk made me a little nervous. Because I felt we could have made the decision for me to drop out of fourth grade and learn everything in the kitchen without him.

"Is reading too advanced too?" my mother asked, squeezing my hand.

I shook my head.

"Mr. Hawk doesn't teach reading. I leave the class and have reading with Ms. Golden. Because I'm in gifted reading, remember?" I asked.

It made me sad to think that my mother had forgotten that I was in gifted reading with Ms. Golden. Because I was very proud of that fact. Because I was in there with all the smart kids.

"But you like Ms. Golden, right?" my mother asked.

"Yes," I said. "But I only see her three times a week."

Talking about school made me realize how Sally-less and awful it was, and I started sniffling.

"Is there something else?" my mother asked.

I nodded.

"What?"

"PE," I said.

"What about it?" my mother asked. "You've never said anything about not liking PE before."

I sniffled really hard.

"Well, lately, we've been playing dodgeball. Except some of the kids call it slaughterball, and sometimes they try to hit certain people in the head."

My mother gasped.

"So Mr. Hawk doesn't teach you any reading at all and he makes you learn sixth-grade math and science?" my mother asked. "And for PE he lets the other children throw balls at your head?"

I almost nodded, but I wasn't sure if what my mother was saying was the exact truth. It sounded pretty severe.

"I don't know if everything we learn is sixth grade. But it feels very advanced." I sniffled. "And he doesn't *want* the other kids to throw the balls directly at our heads. But it does happen."

"Unbelievable!" my mother said. "Well, I'm going to take you to school on Monday and have a talk with him about this."

"Um," I said. "Okay."

So I sat at the kitchen table and read all about laws.

And how the basic purpose of a government was to make laws, carry out laws, and decide if laws had been broken. And how equality under the law meant that all people were treated fairly. Which was a nice idea, but I didn't think that it happened all the time.

After I finished with social studies, I put my head down on the table.

"Do you need a break?" my mother asked.

This made me jump a little, because I hadn't known she was still in the kitchen.

"Yes," I said. "But I don't want more cheese."

"Should we call Aunt Stella in Modesto?" my mother asked.

"Yes! Yes!" I said, because I loved talking to Aunt Stella. In fact, I loved talking to Aunt Stella in Modesto so much, that the month after Sally moved, I called Aunt Stella thirty-seven times. And talked for over nine hundred minutes. And got banned from using the phone to make long-distance calls ever again. Except in the case of what my parents called a grave emergency.

My mother dialed my aunt Stella on the kitchen phone and then handed it to me.

"Aunt Stella! It's Camille! How's Modesto?" I asked.

"Camille, how are you? Does your mother know that you're calling me?"

Then something terrible happened. My mother pushed a button and put the call on speakerphone. So I couldn't tell Aunt Stella anything personal. I could only tell her things that I could tell my mother.

"I'm here too, Stella," my mother said.

"How's school?" Aunt Stella asked.

But before I could say anything about school, my mother started talking about how my teacher was science-centered, extremely challenging, and a promoter of sports violence.

I stood and listened. And I felt pretty bad. Because I didn't think Mr. Hawk was a bad teacher. I just would have preferred to learn in my own kitchen.

I sat down and listened to my mom and Aunt Stella talk. One of the things I liked about Aunt Stella was that she was from California, and that place had an ocean. Where I lived in Idaho there weren't any oceans. Only lakes. And things called reservoirs that looked like lakes, but they were actually built by people to store water. And while it was common to see people waterskiing in them, if a reservoir ever broke, which could happen, the water would flood towns and kill everybody and their dogs.

"Camille, are you still there?" Aunt Stella asked.

"Yes," I said.

"Well, you and your family are going to have to come visit me," she said.

"And drive to the ocean?" I asked.

I really wanted to wear my swimsuit in the ocean.

Because Idaho had dangerous rivers, and streams, and irrigation canals, but none of those things had waves. Just deadly currents.

"Of course we can drive to the ocean," Aunt Stella said.

Then she said she loved me and I said I loved her and my mother hung up the phone. Even though we didn't have a firm date, thinking about my trip to California made me smile. I now felt good enough to attempt math. I took out my worksheets and looked at them. I was at the point where I had to times everything by nine. Even other nines. I took a deep breath. I found timesing things by nine to be hard work. I tapped my finger to help me count and I scribbled answers. When I finished those, I drank some water. Then I had spelling words. They were all trick words that sounded alike. I didn't like words like that. I thought maybe the government should have made a law against these kinds of words: *threw, through; close, clothes; sure, shore; would, wood.*

My mother looked over my shoulder.

"You're studying homophones?" she asked me.

"I guess," I said.

Then my mom called Aunt Stella again and started complaining about how advanced homophones were. For some reason, this made my head itch, so I scratched it. After talking about homophones, my mom started talking about carpet. She was so happy her voice sounded like it was singing. This made me look at the walls. They were too purple to try to study spelling in the kitchen anymore. I grabbed all my homework and hugged it to me.

"Where are you going?" my mother asked.

"My room," I said.

I walked down the purple hallway and locked eyes on my purple door. Inside, my room was still painted its normal color: white with some dirt smudges. I sat on my bed and finished my homework and tried not to listen to my mom talking to Aunt Stella about essential home repairs. Because I knew that painting your house purple was not an essential home repair. Then I heard her hang up. And walk down the hallway to my room.

"I think we should have vegetarian lasagna for dinner," my mother said.

"Does it have eggplant in it?" I asked.

"No. Why do you always ask about eggplant? You've only eaten it one time."

I lifted my finger in the air.

"I only needed to eat it one time," I said.

My mother put her hands on her hips.

"When it comes to eggplant, I think you're being a little unfair," my mother said. "Eggplant isn't evil. In fact, the paint I chose for the house is called Majestic Eggplant."

That's when my mouth dropped open. I hadn't realized this, but our house did look exactly like an eggplant. This was so terrible. My head felt dizzy, and I lay down. My books and papers slid off my bed and crashed sloppily to the floor.

"I feel very doomed," I said.

"Don't worry, Camille. I'll drive you to school and talk with Mr. Hawk first thing tomorrow morning." She leaned down and kissed me. "You're not doomed. You're a McPhee."

But staring up at my ceiling, I couldn't see the difference.

CHAPTER 7

MY blue butteRFly

"I can't drive you today, because I have to teach aerobics," my mother said.

It was Monday. I sat at the kitchen table eating my cereal.

"The gym just called and the regular instructor aggravated her shin splints. It looks like I'll be teaching this class for a while."

My mother sat down next to me looking very thrilled.

"It's an advanced abdominals class, which mainly

utilizes inflatable balance balls. It's a fantastic opportunity for me to learn more ball work."

"Ball work?" I echoed.

My mother stood up and placed her hands on her newly flattened stomach.

"Ball work targets the core like you wouldn't believe," she said. "In fact, modified ball work replaces a lot of outdated moves—sit-ups, push-ups, leg lifts, the plow." My mother shook her head. "If women understood how overrated sit-ups were, they'd embrace the ball in a heartbeat."

I sighed. Then I set my spoon down next to my bowl. And I lovingly touched the kitchen table.

"I think school is overrated," I said. "And this spot would be a great place for me to learn everything. Math. Social studies. Science—"

My mother cut me off.

"Camille, you're not getting homeschooled at the kitchen table. But don't worry. I'll visit Mr. Hawk soon and have a talk with him about toning down the advanced material."

My mother swept her hair back into a ponytail.

"Hurry up!" she said. "You don't want to miss the bus."

I carried my bowl to the sink.

Yes, I do want to miss the bus, I thought. *Yes, I do!*

Outside, the whole world felt like a Popsicle. I set

my cooler down in its usual spot and tried not to listen to anybody. Manny and Danny kept telling me to watch my step. And Polly never looked at me. When the bus finally rolled to a stop, I crossed in front of it at a very slow rate of speed. At the top of the stairs, Mrs. Spittle put her hand out and made me wait. She wanted to remind me that she hadn't run over me and that I shouldn't tell people that she had.

"I wouldn't tell people that," I said.

"Good. Because there's a big difference between being struck by the bus and having a little slip near the bus," she said.

"I believe you," I said.

"Good. Because school officials view driving over the students as a serious offense," she said.

I found an empty seat near the front of the bus and acted like a dingo. Which meant not listening to all the kids on the bus laugh at me. Also, I scratched behind my ears. And I did a little growling. I made a mental note to myself that I would never laugh at anyone who fell down ever again. Even if somebody I didn't like slipped on a banana peel and fell headfirst into a toilet. Instead of laughing at that person, I would try to be like Sally and help the person out.

Class started with math. I thought we'd talk about how to times numbers by nine. But we were already on to something else. Mr. Hawk stood in front of us and turned a piece of chalk on the blackboard like it was a screw. He made a perfect point. You might be thinking that Mr. Hawk looked like a hawk, but he didn't. He looked like an eagle. He had shiny gray hair that he liked to slick back, and he had a great big nose that was quite long and drooped down, almost touching his lips. And when he lifted his long arms, it looked like he was raising a big, featherless wing.

As I sat and learned about how decimal points changed my understanding of how numbers worked, I felt somebody pushing their eraser tip into my shoulder blade. It was Tony Maboney. I did not enjoy sitting in front of Tony Maboney. Because not only was he a pain in the neck, he had also become a pain in my shoulder blade. Every time Mr. Hawk said the word *point*, Tony Maboney poked me with his pencil. I felt like flipping around and asking Tony Maboney, "What's your problem?" But I didn't do that. Instead, I asked myself, *What would a dingo do*? And I realized that the answer to this question was simple. *Nothing*. A dingo wouldn't react. So that's what I did. I sat there very content.

Finally, in an attempt to emotionally wound me with his slobber, Tony shot a spit wad at me. He launched the wet papery ball so fast that it ricocheted off my thick hair and into the stringy hair of Polly Clausen. Polly used her pencil to flick it out of her hair and onto the floor.

Then Tony leaned forward and whispered into my ear. "Camille, I've got a pig on my farm just like you. It's skinny and stupid and has a big head and it keeps falling down."

Then he started to snort like a pig.

I wanted to point out to Tony that I did not have a big head. I just had terrific hair. And that I'd only fallen underneath a school bus once. And that it was actually very easy to do, because school buses are big. And we're always walking in front of them. Anyone can slip on a stupid patch of ice.

Sadly, right before Tony said this, my legs were feeling wobbly and I was going to eat a ham sandwich. But I knew that when somebody was calling you a pig and snorting, it wasn't the best time to open up your cooler and chow down on a pork product.

What Tony Maboney said really bothered me. But I couldn't let him see that. Even though it was hard, I had to tune him out. I knew that if my face had gotten red, or if I had released even the tiniest sniffle, Tony Maboney would have called me oinker, hoofy, or snout-face for the next nine years. You have to be smarter than the bullies. Luckily, bullies aren't always the sharpest crayons in the box.

All through math, I worked on decimal problems. I even went on to a chapter that wasn't assigned. It was very advanced and it started to blow my mind. Then I made the mistake of looking up. I did not sit in a good seat for looking up. I sat below a huge, dangling hornet. It was made out of construction paper and pipe cleaners and some sort of fake fur. Mr. Hawk loved insects. I think they were his favorite animal.

When he'd taught sixth grade, he'd assigned his class to make giant bugs out of what he called "affordable craft items from home." After the project, he would hang all the insects on wires. And he never took them down. He had been giving this assignment for a long time, because his classroom ceiling dripped with bugs. And some of them were pretty low-hanging. Like my hornet. I couldn't believe how ugly a hornet's belly was. It was a miserable thing to be stuck beneath. Polly got to sit under a ladybug. Tony was seated below a dragonfly. Nina Hosack, the class wimp, got to sit under a bright, happy firefly. I would have preferred any of those insects. Because they didn't hang low. Or have scary eyes. Or a dangerous hind end.

Mr. Hawk had not assigned us our insects yet. But I already knew what I was going to make. I was going to make a big blue butterfly. Because those insects were beautiful and never tried to sting anybody's eyes out. Unlike hornets, which were a kind of wasp. They hatched from their eggs angry and trying to sting people's eyes out right away.

After math there was social studies. Mr. Hawk talked a lot about laws and there was even a discussion about how our class should write our own constitution. But I thought this was a terrible idea. Because I didn't trust some of these clowns, and I didn't want to have to follow their laws. Especially Tony Maboney. Social studies made me do a lot of yawning. I ate some granola to stay awake. Then came lunch. And I wasn't totally hungry. So I asked Mr. Hawk if I could stay at my desk and work on a project. Or maybe watch the hermit crab in the back of the room.

"Everybody has to go to the cafeteria, Camille," he said.

This made me very sad. But I did it anyway. On my way, I passed two third graders in the hallway coming back from lunch. At Rocky Mountain Elementary School we ate in two shifts. The first graders through third graders ate first. Then the fourth graders through sixth graders went next. Because if the lunch ladies tried to serve the whole school pizza or tacos at the same time, some of the food would have gotten cold, and grown poisonous bacteria, and made everybody who ate it too sick to learn for at least a week.

I ate at one of the fourth-grade tables. There were

twice as many fourth graders than any other grade. So we got two tables. I liked to sit with my back to the wall so I could watch the fifth and sixth graders. Because some of the older boys were crazy and liked to throw food at each other. And sometimes they missed their mark and a third grader got peas or applesauce stuck in her hair. And I would rather duck than have that happen.

I tried not to think about the decimal point and sat next to Lilly Poe. But I didn't talk to her. Even though sometimes our shoulders touched. I did talk a little bit to Gracie Clop. But I mostly listened to her tell a story about how she had the best grandpa in the world. Because he'd fed gumdrops to a grizzly bear in Yellowstone Park. And she had the pictures to prove it.

I didn't have any living grandparents. Grandpa and Grandma McPhee died before I was born. And Grandma Denny died when I was a baby. And Grandpa Denny died when I was three. I've seen pictures of me sitting on his lap, but I can't remember him. He does look very familiar, though. And we still have the chair that he was sitting on in the photographs. Gracie promised to bring us pictures of her grandpa feeding that bear. Everybody seemed very thrilled about seeing them.

"That's crazy," Lilly Poe said. "Bring them tomorrow."

"Do you think grizzly bears like chocolate chip cookies?" Zoey Combs asked, stuffing the last of one in her mouth.

"Bears eat anything. Even garbage," Tony Maboney said.

And then everybody started talking about the grossest sandwich a bear would eat, mostly involving trash. But I wasn't curious about what kind of trash sandwich a bear would eat. Because I was thinking about all my grandparents. If they were still here, I didn't think that I'd want them to go around feeding gumdrops to grizzly bears. No, I'd want my grandparents to forget about grizzly bears and spend a bunch of time with me. And maybe feed *me* gumdrops.

Looking around the cafeteria made me very sad. I didn't understand how so many unfair things could happen to one person. Who decided that I shouldn't have grandparents? My mind spun around in circles trying to find a way to make things feel less awful. But I couldn't figure it out. Because there was no way I would ever get the chance to know them. And there was no way they would ever get the chance to know me.

I wiped my mouth with my napkin, packed up my cooler, and walked back to class.

CHAPTER 8

LEGENDS

One thing that was fair about fourth grade was that after lunch, on Monday, Wednesday, and Friday, I got to go to gifted reading. And the great thing about gifted reading was that I had to leave my classroom and sit in the back corner of another classroom where there were beanbag chairs. That's where I always chose to sit. There were eight of us in gifted reading, and only five beanbag chairs. So some of the other kids sat on the floor. But they didn't seem to mind. And I didn't understand the logic of that. Because you can sit on the floor whenever you want. But you can only sit in a beanbag chair when they happen to be available.

Ms. Golden asked us to sit in our usual circle and then she brought out the book we were reading about myths and legends. We read a story called "The Sedna Legend." It was the story of Sedna, an Eskimo sea goddess. It told about how all the sea animals came into existence. I thought it was a pretty wild story. But Polly liked it quite a bit. And so did Lilly Poe. And Boone Berry. And even Nina Hosack. Which surprised me a great deal, because the story had blood in it. When we got to that part, I thought Nina was going to pass out or start crying for the nurse. But she didn't. She just made a squeaky sound and turned the page.

Except for the seals, I was mostly neutral about Sedna's story. And so were the other three readers—Penny Winchester, Duncan Cole, and Jory Bennett. We liked the story okay, but we weren't in love with it. I'd read better legends. "How the Coyote Danced with the Blackbirds" and "Why the Ant Is Almost Cut in Two" were two of my favorite legends we'd read in gifted reading. In fact, I liked them so much, I was secretly hoping we'd read them again.

"Sedna must have been so scared," Polly said.

I rolled my eyes. And Polly saw me. And so did Lilly Poe. And she rolled her eyes right back at me. And then I felt bad.

"Who wants to summarize the story?" Ms. Golden asked. Her hair was looking extra bright and wonderful that day and I thought it smelled like sugar cookies.

"I do! I do!" Penny said.

Ms. Golden pointed to Penny and that released a flood of words.

"Sedna was a girl who went off to live with a guy on an island. But then the guy turned out not to be a guy but a bird. Then Sedna felt betrayed by this and tried to escape with her father, but the sea went crazy and Sedna's father had to throw her into it to calm it down."

Penny shook her head and twisted some of her long brown hair around her finger. "I know. I know. Isn't that crazy that he threw his own daughter into the water like that?" Then she shook her head some more and kept going. "Then Sedna tried to get back in the boat and her dad was really scared and so he stabbed her hands and then Sedna's blood turned into all kinds of sea creatures, like seals and whales." Penny looked up at us, horrified. "Her own father stabbed her! Can you believe it?"

"My dad would never stab me," Lilly said. "Even if it meant that our ship would sink."

I watched Polly turn and look out the window. This was probably not the best story for her to read. Because it had a dad in it. And that's what she was missing in life.

"I don't think anybody's father would really stab them," I said. "I think that's what makes this a legend."

But then Jory shot up his hand and said, "Sedna's father should have been arrested."

Then Ms. Golden smiled at us and closed the book and told everybody to take a deep breath. We did.

"Let's all come to the table and do some active reflecting," she said.

I got out of my beanbag chair and sat at the small art table where we did our "active reflecting." Ms. Golden handed us two sheets of paper. Each one had the outline of a head on it. The inside of the head was blank.

"One head is Sedna's. And the other head is her father's. I want you to think about how they must've been feeling during the storm. Using pictures, go ahead and put their thoughts inside their heads. You have some time to get started. Bring them with you on Wednesday."

I took my two blank heads and started drawing life jackets inside both of them right away. Because I thought that's what a person would think about when they were going to drown. I pushed so hard on my orange crayon that it started to crumble. That's when I looked over at Polly. She was drawing something complicated. In Sedna's head, she was drawing a man. And in Sedna's father's head, she was drawing a girl. I guess

Polly thought that during the storm they would've been thinking about each other. That made sense. But I decided not to copy her and stick with my life jackets. Because my idea made sense too.

After gifted reading, we went back to Mr. Hawk's room and studied science. I ate two pieces of thin-sliced ham while Mr. Hawk talked about hazardous waste. And how gasoline should never get spilled onto the ground. And he talked about the difference between an open dump and a sanitary landfill. I didn't know that a sanitary landfill meant that the garbage got crushed and layered and covered with a coat of dirt.

Mr. Hawk said it was a better way to throw things away than to toss them in open dumps, because open dumps had problems with insects and rodents and were fire hazards. Also, the wind could blow the trash around, and that's not ideal. After hearing this, I decided not to eat a third piece of ham. And for PE, Mr. Hawk said that it was okay if I stayed in the classroom, and this thrilled me very much. Because I got to watch the hermit crab. His name was Herman. And he didn't do much. But that was okay. Waiting for Herman to do something was sort of fun too.

After class, I packed up my things and headed out to the bus. But I only made it halfway. I saw my dad's black Mazda pickup parked in the school's parking lot. He beeped his horn at me and waved his arm out the window. I was both happy and worried. What if he'd been home and seen the house? What if he was so mad that he wanted to turn me into a double agent and plot revenge against my mother? What if I had to choose between my parents? *What if?*

But my dad was smiling wide. Even from so far away, I could see his teeth sparkle behind the bug-splattered windshield. He looked happy. Clearly, he hadn't entered our Majestic Eggplant house yet.

When I crawled into the pickup, he squeezed my knee and asked me if I wanted to go get pizza. I smiled. Ever since my mother started teaching aerobics, pizza was a banned food item in our house. So were Twinkies, nachos, whole milk, licorice, French fries, French toast, fried chicken, red meat, Pop-Tarts, white bread, white rice, doughnuts, ice cream, all gummy products, potato chips, cheese puffs, enchiladas, and egg yolks. When she made us scrambled eggs for breakfast, she only used egg whites. They looked like a pile of flat cotton sprinkled with little black pepper flakes. But when I closed my eyes and chewed them, they tasted quite a bit like eggs.

My dad had been in Seattle for a whole week. And I had missed him a lot. The longest he'd ever been gone was two weeks. My mom and dad had an agreement that he could never be gone longer than that. Because not seeing each other for three weeks wasn't good for married people.

When we got to the pizza parlor, my father let me order a triple-meat pepperoni pizza. The meat slices held little puddles of grease in their centers.

"We should blot it," my father said. He wadded up some extra napkins and lightly pressed them against our pizza. Tons of grease stuck to them, turning the napkins a bright orange, greasy color.

"We've reduced the fat," he said, smiling again. "Your mother would be proud."

This made me laugh.

"So, what interesting things happened while I was gone?" he asked.

"Um nuh fuff," I mumbled, cramming pizza in my mouth with both hands, hoping to fill it so full that it would make it impossible for me to talk.

"Yeah," he said smiling. "I miss pizza too."

I nodded with lots of enthusiasm. My hair bounced around my face like it was part human and part kangaroo.

"Watch it," he said. "You don't want to choke."

I stuffed down another slice of pizza and drank a large root beer. It worked. I kept my mouth so full that I never had to respond to questions that might have led to dangerous answers.

When we turned into our driveway, I thought I was going to hurl my pizza back up. My father reached behind him and pulled out a brand-new toilet seat.

"Think she'll like it?" he asked. "It's got twice as much cushion as the leading cushioned seat."

My father was hurting my heart. He had no idea what was waiting for him on the other side of that door.

I walked behind him—slowly. He bounded up the front steps in one giant leap and threw open the door.

"I'm home!" he called, rushing inside. "What is this?" he asked. "Where am I?" The toilet seat slipped from his hand and landed upside down on the new plush carpet.

"Don't expect life to be fair," I mumbled.

But I don't think he heard me. He blinked and blinked and blinked, like bugs had flown into both his eyes. Then he stood motionless. He squeezed his lips together so tight that his mouth didn't look like a mouth anymore.

There was a new, cross-stitched sign hanging on the wall:

PLEASE TAKE YOUR SHOES OFF AT THE DOOR
SO WE CAN KEEP A SPOTLESS FLOOR.

I didn't want to mark up the new carpet, so I went ahead and slipped off my shoes. But my father didn't.

He pulled the sign down from the wall and tossed it on the couch.

"It's just her midlife crisis. Don't take it personally," I reminded him. But he wasn't listening to me. He was exploding.

"Midlife crisis, my butt. We can't afford this. It'll put us right back in the hole! Maxine," he said, charging toward the kitchen. "I refuse to live in a grape!"

CHAPTER 9

PEACE & BANANAS

That night, my parents fought long and hard. I went downstairs to the basement family room to watch TV. I didn't love the basement family room, because it was unfinished. Basically, it was a cement floor with a rug on it. And a couch with uncomfortable springs. And the walls weren't even solid yet. I could see pink insulation and wood beams and pipes. And every time I saw this, I felt like I was looking at my house's guts. And that wasn't pleasant. Also, there wasn't much light down there. But the basement family room was the farthest away from my fighting parents that I could get. So that's where I went.

I turned on the TV and watched a show about a wolverine attacking another wolverine. They bit at each other's ears, clawed at each other's bellies, and tore at each other's throats for what seemed like hours. They showed no mercy. The wildlife expert said that the wolverine was the most ferocious animal in the wild kingdom. And after seeing what I saw, I believed this statement.

When I went upstairs to get a banana, I noticed that the way my parents fought reminded me a lot of those wolverines. They weren't actually biting each other, though. They used words. And the words that flew out of their mouths were horrible and mean.

I took my banana and went to my bedroom. I curled up under my covers and listened. I wanted a referee to show up and stand between them and blow his whistle. In first grade, Penny Winchester and I got in a fight on the playground over a pale pink rock. I *found* it, but she said that she *saw* it first. She ended up pulling my hair. I ended up pulling hers back.

We were sent to the teachers' lounge to talk to Mrs. Moses. The vice principal called it mediation. Mrs. Moses was very wise. She put the rock on the table in front of us and said that she was going to break it in two so that we each could have a part of it. That sounded good to me and Penny. Mrs. Moses got a hammer and held it over her head.

"I would expect that the real owner of this little, pink baby rock would want it to remain whole," she said, looking first at me and then at Penny.

But we both shrugged and told her to whack it.

She seemed really disappointed.

"I guess I'll cut your precious baby rock in half," she said, bringing the hammer down hard.

She actually broke it into eight pieces and some dust. Penny took four pieces and I took four pieces and we left the dust and were both happy. I needed somebody as smart as Mrs. Moses to come over here and cut the house in half, or the toilet seat in half, or the hole in half, and fix this situation.

My parents probably would have fought all night. But then I realized something. I considered what was happening between those two to be a "grave emergency." So I called Aunt Stella.

"Camille, it's late," Aunt Stella said. "Does your mother know you're calling me?"

"No. She's fighting with my dad," I said.

"Oh," she said. "Are you crying?" she asked.

"Uh-huh," I said.

"I wish I was there," she said. "I'd give you a big hug."

"Mom painted the whole house Majestic Eggplant and now Dad is exploding," I said.

"That doesn't sound good. But they can't fight forever. Eventually they'll stop," she said.

I thought about telling Aunt Stella that sometimes wolverines didn't stop fighting until one of them was dead.

"We're trying to stay out of the hole," I said. "But Mom bought new carpet. For the whole house. And then she sprung it on Dad like it was a great surprise. But it wasn't."

"Oh dear," she said.

"I think we're back in the hole again," I said.

"Camille, you shouldn't worry about money. You're ten," Aunt Stella said. "Do you want me to talk to them?"

"They're too busy fighting to talk right now," I said.

"I'm very disappointed in them. They're adults. They need to keep their domestic problems to themselves," Aunt Stella said.

"I think they need mediation," I said.

Aunt Stella laughed. "Who doesn't?"

"I better go," I said.

"You can call me any time," Aunt Stella said.

"But I'm only allowed to phone you if it's a grave emergency."

"Camille, you can call me whenever you want. Even in the middle of the night."

"Okay," I said. "But that's usually when I'm sleeping."

"What I mean is that I'm always here for you," she said.

And hearing Aunt Stella say this made me feel very good. But it also made me cry more.

After I hung up with Aunt Stella, my parents kept fighting. It was terrible. I had to do something. My entire body was feeling quaking sad. So I ran out of my room and said, "You need mediation!"

They both looked at me. Then they looked at each other. And I thought their faces appeared very ashamed.

"Seriously. It's very hard for me to hear these things," I said. "You're parents, not wolverines."

Then I went back to my bedroom and I didn't hear any more yelling. In fact, I heard my mother agree to help my father repaint the house. And I heard my father admit that he actually liked the new carpet. And I heard both my parents come into my room and say that they loved me, right as I was tumbling into sleep.

The next morning when I woke up, the cushioned toilet seat had already been installed. And when I went to school, nobody made fun of me for falling underneath the bus. And Tony Maboney had a temperature and went home early and didn't feel up to poking me in the shoulder before he left. And in the hallway, Ms. Golden complimented me on my fancy socks because they had ruffles on them. And during science, as we learned about how air pollutants affect asthma and can also make it easier for people to catch a cold or the flu, that low-hanging hornet's wire broke and the hornet fell on me.

"It has a dangerous hind end!" I screamed.

"Ah, it broke," Mr. Hawk said, pulling the insect out of my hair.

And it had! That hornet's head came right off its body and landed next to my shoe. Also, I kicked it.

And so Mr. Hawk decided to replace it with a neat-looking cricket.

"Crickets don't sting, right?" I asked. Because I was basically sure, but I wanted to check.

"Right, they sing," he said.

"Sweet," I said, staring up at the new bug.

My day kept getting better and better. For lunch, I ate pizza with sausage on it. And when I got home from school, the meditation wall was already repainted a soft white.

"Hi, honey!" my mom said. She had a paint roller in her hand. "I'm priming."

"Great!" I said.

"Everything will be the color of the meditation wall," she said. "It's called Cotton. Do you like it?"

"Very much," I said.

"Me too," she said. "And so does your father."

But I wasn't surprised. Of course we liked the color Cotton. Everybody likes cotton. Because it's the type of material that doesn't itch or melt in the dryer. Plus, when you make it out of sugar, you can eat it at the zoo.

My house felt very wonderful. And then Mrs. Bratberg called and needed a mother's helper for the next day, which meant more money for my calling card.

As I watched my mother prime the ceiling, I thought about what she'd said about life having ups and downs. Maybe she was right. Maybe life was like a series of mountains. Up and down. Up and down. Maybe somehow all the unfair things and the fair things balanced out.

I walked through my house and fell face-first onto my bed. This was all very marvelous news. In fact, it was so marvelous I thought about calling Aunt Stella and telling her that she had been right. I was ten. I didn't need to worry about money. Or being in the hole. Besides, the hole must not have been as big as my dad thought. My parents had declared a truce! They didn't need mediation after all! This made me feel so fantastic that I decided to go for a walk around my house and celebrate. I grabbed a banana and went to the backyard.

"I'm going outside to do some stuff," I said.

"Wear your gloves," my mother said. "On your hands."

This was a good reminder. Sometimes I kept them tucked inside my pocket.

Even though the ground was snowy, I got down on my hands and knees and crawled around like a very thrilled dingo. That's when I saw something. It was a squirrel. And I'd seen this squirrel before. It had been visiting my window for over a year. It did this for two reasons. One, the squirrel liked me. Two, I often left the squirrel yummy food like popcorn and lunch meat.

That's when I realized something important. This squirrel probably wanted to be my pet. Because it was always looking for me. I squinted to make sure it was the same squirrel I'd been taking care of all year. I remembered it as being fluffier during the summer. But then I realized that squirrels might not look exactly the same all year long. Because they lived in the wild, and those conditions were severe.

The squirrel twitched its tail. It looked cold. But was I really ready for another pet? What if I found Checkers? Would she get along with my new pet squirrel? My dad had told me that I was never going to see Checkers again, due to the fact that she was in heaven. He was firm on this. But my mother always said there was hope. Sometimes, when this topic came up, my father looked out the window and didn't say anything else. I guess he didn't like talking about heaven. Even though, from what I heard, it sounded like a pretty fantastic place. Except for the fact that you had to be dead to get there. The squirrel stood up very straight and froze. It had cute ears. I decided to name it Rhonda.

Since squirrels are such excellent runners, I stood up too. Because chasing my new pet squirrel Rhonda on my hands and knees would have meant losing my new pet squirrel. She crouched down again. I made sure my gloves were on tight and lifted up my hands. She was investigating something in the low branches of the yew bush beneath my window. I sneaked closer. The cold kept making Rhonda twitch. I knew she would be very grateful to live in my house.

"Rhonda," I sweetly called. "Welcome to your new, warm home."

That's when I learned many terrible things about Rhonda. First, she wasn't very grateful after all. Second, she was evil. And one of the things that made Rhonda evil was that she was an unkind mammal. Rhonda turned around and ran toward me. She was acting like she wanted to bite me. Maybe to death. That's when I pictured heaven and ran very fast.

It was awful.

"I don't want you anymore," I said. "Go away!"

I hoped the evil squirrel would run up a tree. But it didn't want to do that. Because it was evil. The squirrel followed me into the front yard. And made barking sounds. It was a pretty rude squirrel, too. I think I was screaming really loud, because Polly came running over.

"Are you okay?" she asked.

"That evil squirrel isn't grateful at all. It hates me!" I said.

"What evil squirrel?" Polly asked. "Are you playing a game?"

I thought her questions were pretty dumb. First, I was not okay. I was sweating. Second, there was no such game as running away from an evil squirrel. And even if there was, there's no way I could've been playing it, because I was screaming for real, and when I played games, I didn't scream for real. But when I turned to point at the evil squirrel, it had totally disappeared. I hated that thing.

"It was right there," I said, pointing to an empty patch of snow. "Look, you can see its tracks."

"I don't need to see its tracks," Polly said. "I believe you."

Then she did this awful thing. I was totally unprepared for it. Polly smiled at me. I didn't want her to do that. Why did she think I wanted her to do that? What was wrong with her?

"Do you want to come over and paint?" she asked.

This offer was more awful than the first awful thing and way more awful than that evil squirrel. I didn't know what to say. The silence lasted a long time. Her smile melted. Then the sad Polly face I was used to seeing at the bus stop returned.

"Maybe another time," she said.

I watched her leave. I watched her hurry across my yard and hers. I watched her climb her cement steps and go back inside her house. I watched her stringy-haired head move past her living room window as she disappeared into a room deep inside her home. I let out a big sigh. I think it was mostly filled with relief. I didn't need a friend. I needed an international calling card. And I hoped that Polly could understand that.

CHAPTER 10

AVOID THE SPARK

When I woke up the next day, I couldn't stop thinking about quarters. I really liked quarters. Maybe *too* much. Because out of the fifty dollars that I'd saved, almost all of it was in quarters. And those things are heavy, and if I was serious about buying an international calling card, I was going to need to pay for it in bills. If I didn't, people in line behind me would hate me. And when people in line behind me hated me, it made me feel rotten.

I thought a good person to talk to about this was

Mrs. Bratberg. Because she was the person who was paying me in quarters. Because I had told her many times that I preferred quarters to everything. I called her on the phone, and she was very nice about my idea.

"I would like to be paid in bills today," I said.

"Okay," she said.

"Also, I have too many quarters. I need to turn them into bills."

"Bring them over," she said. "I can use them to teach Dustin a practical lesson in math."

Before I went over to the Bratbergs', I put all of my change in one of my dad's socks and put that sock in my coat pocket. I also packed my cooler and said goodbye to my mother.

"Don't tell your father," she said.

"I won't."

My dad was on a business trip in Utah. Which worked out for me. As I walked over to the Bratbergs', I did a little bit of looking for Checkers. I also did some looking for that evil squirrel. But I didn't see either. I also stopped by my mother's old Chevy, because I had been finding lots of change in there. Mostly in her ashtray.

But I didn't find any change in there that day. Instead, I found a note:

Camille, stop taking all my change. I use it to pay the parking meters in town.

Without any quarters, I'm going to get a ticket.

This note made me feel pretty bad. So I opened up my sock and gave my mom two quarters. Then I found a pen and wrote:

Here you go, Mom. Enjoy my quarters.

When I got to the Bratbergs', I learned some good and some bad news. First, Brody had a sprained ankle and wasn't allowed to get out of bed for anything. Except to use the bathroom. That meant I only had to focus on the other two Bratbergs. Then, Mrs. Bratberg told me the bad news.

"Camille," she said, grabbing her coat. "There's been an incident."

"Does that mean you don't need a mother's helper today?" I asked. I didn't understand why she'd put on her coat. I didn't think their house was cold.

"The post office just called me. I made a mistake on postage, so they're holding my packages. If I don't go down there and take care of it right now, my shipments won't go out today. Do you know what that will do to my seller's-reputation score?"

"Lower it?" I asked.

"Exactly," Mrs. Bratberg said.

"So we're going to the post office?" I asked.

She shook her head.

"Camille, I need to ask you to do something that I don't normally ask you to do." She placed one hand heavily on my shoulder.

"What is it?" I asked.

"Just for today, for the next hour, I need you to be more than a mother's helper. I need you to be a babysitter."

"A babysitter?" I asked. I didn't think I'd be one of those until I was in high school.

"You've got my cell phone number," she said, picking up her purse. "What do you think? Can you do it?"

I glanced at Samantha and Dustin. Then I looked back at Mrs. Bratberg.

"I'll pay you double," Mrs. Bratberg said.

I heard myself say, "Okay."

"I'll be back in one hour," she said. "Except it might take an hour and a half." Then she slammed the door.

"See you," I said. But the door was already closed.

After Mrs. Bratberg left, I decided to lay down the law with Samantha and Dustin.

"You are not allowed to take your turtle out of its aquarium," I said.

They nodded.

"And you can't put your underpants in the

microwave. Or touch any glue. And nobody is allowed to put anybody in a plastic bag."

"We won't," Samantha said.

"Today, I'm the babysitter," I said.

Samantha and Dustin smiled at me.

"Okay," Dustin said.

I was relieved to hear them agree with me so quickly. They were pretty good at keeping their word. I let out a deep breath. Then I checked on Brody. Peeking through the crack of his barely open bedroom door, I saw his foot resting on a stack of pillows. He didn't look like he was going anywhere. Even to the bathroom. So I shut the door, found some snacks, took my sock (because I didn't want to leave it unattended), grabbed the remote control, and found a comfortable place to sit.

"Can we go outside?" Samantha asked. She was wearing a big, red, puffy coat zipped to her chin. She'd wrapped her scarf around her head, leaving only her dark brown eyes showing.

"It's cold out," I said, tossing potato chips into my mouth. I was comfortably seated in the middle of their enormous beanbag. And I'd turned on the Science Channel. A badger was chewing on a rotten log. Inside, he had found a thick wall of honeycomb. Bees were stinging him like crazy.

"I'll only be out for five minutes," she said, batting her eyelashes at me.

"Where's Dustin?" I asked.

"He'll come too," she said, slipping on her gloves.

I didn't think it was a great idea, but I didn't think it was the worst idea in the world either. Because their turtle was inside. And so was the microwave. And their underpants. And all their glue. And everything else that was off-limits.

"Don't you want to watch the badger?" I asked. I pointed to the screen. That badger had a real sweet tooth. Even when the bees stung his pink gums, he kept biting at the log.

Samantha looked at the TV and shook her head. "No," she said.

"Five minutes," I said.

I heard her boots pound down the hall. Had I been listening more closely, I would have realized that I heard one set of boots thumping out the door, and one set of boots being dragged out the door.

You'd think that I would have gotten tired of watching that badger eat honey. But I didn't. When Samantha came back inside, I knew that she had been gone for a lot longer than five minutes.

"Your face is really red," I said. "You should come sit down and watch this badger." She stared at me hard, unblinking.

"I guess we can watch something else," I said, reaching for the remote. "Go get Dustin."

Samantha didn't move.

"I can't," she said, speaking through her scarf.

"Why not?" I asked, rolling off the beanbag onto my hands and knees.

"Because I don't have the key." Her brown eyes had grown very big.

"What key?" I asked.

"The Halloween key," she said. One perfect tear rolled out of her eye and dripped onto her coat.

"Did you lock him in a pumpkin or something?"

She didn't answer. Then I remembered. For Halloween all three of them had dressed up as sheriffs, and all three of them had handcuffs.

"Does this involve handcuffs?" I asked, grabbing her by the shoulders.

"After you arrest your bandits you have to cuff them."

My mouth dropped open.

"You cuff them and then you stuff them," she said.

When you're the babysitter, this is terrible news to hear. I left my change sock, threw on my coat, and ran outside. In the backyard, I could see a navy blue figure huddled beside the Bratbergs' propane tank. My stomach flipped. They had a very big propane tank. It's what they used to heat their whole house. "I hate being the bandit!" Dustin said, yanking on the handcuffs.

Samantha had tightly clamped the cuff around Dustin's right wrist, fastening him to the tank's curved metal handle. Even after I took off his glove, there was no way to slip the cuff over his hand. Snot rolled like a little stream out of his nose. He swept his tongue across his upper lip, steering the stream into his mouth.

"You're not going to die. So there's no need to eat your own snot," I said. "I'll get my mom. We have a saw."

I turned to run, but Dustin tugged on my coat.

"If you saw metal, you'll make a spark. I'm attached to a fuel tank," he said. "What if you blow me up? Or send me to the moon?"

He made a good point.

"When's the last time you had your tank filled?" I asked.

"Just yesterday," he said, gulping down air.

"Are you sure?" I asked. Because I thought maybe he was trying to make the situation sound more dramatic. And as the babysitter, I thought the situation sounded plenty dramatic already.

"I'm very sure. It was part of my math lesson. This tank is eighty percent full. Which is the limit. You can only fill a propane tank to eighty percent. Gases can expand as temperatures change."

"I'm aware that gas expands," I said. "When it comes to science, my teacher is very advanced."

Dustin took a deep breath and made more gulping sounds.

"Well, this is a five-hundred-gallon tank. I know, because I had to calculate how many gallons it would take to fill it."

"You can do that in your head?" I asked.

"No, I used a pencil and paper."

Wow. Maybe learning math at home was just as good as learning it at school, because that was a tough problem to solve. I couldn't have done it.

"Are you sure you don't have a key?" I asked Samantha.

"To make sure none of them got into the wrong hands, after Halloween I smeared the keys with peanut butter and fed them to three different neighborhood dogs."

"What?" I cried. "You could have killed them!"

"But I didn't," she said, slowly shaking her head. "Because they're all still running around."

For a moment, I thought about searching for dog turds. But the ground was snow-covered and it was almost March. Even with three dogs out there, the odds that I could find a five-month-old, frozen dog turd with a handcuff key in it seemed pretty slim.

I threw open my front door and cried for my mother. But the sound of my voice echoed through the empty house. I ran to the garage and the car was gone. On the kitchen table was a note.

Had to teach ab blast class. It was an
emergency. Be back soon—with veggie
burgers. I'll probably be back before you.
But you have my number just in case.

When I tried to call her cell phone, it said she was
out of range. When I tried to call the gym, they put me
on hold. And when I tried to call Mrs. Bratberg's cell
phone, all I got was her voice mail. I thought about
calling Aunt Stella, but she lived in Modesto, and I
knew she couldn't help me. Besides that, she was probably working. In a perfect world, I could have called
my very good friend Sally and she would've brought
me a bobby pin and helped me pick the lock. Or I
could have called my father. Problems like this were
right up his alley. But I knew that I couldn't. Being a
mother's helper was a secret. And babysitting? If I told
my father the truth, he'd explode. First at me. Then at
my mother.

At this moment, I realized how unfair it was to live
in a world where people could move to Japan, and
perfectly normal kids could have exploding fathers,
and mothers who turned forty and went to teach an
ab blast class out of range. And aunts who lived in
Modesto and worked day shifts at hospitals.

Sweat rolled down my back. I ran my fingers
through my hair. Then I bit my fingernails. From the

kitchen window, I could see Samantha hopping around her handcuffed brother. This was a serious problem, and I didn't have any answers. I tried to bite my fingernails some more, but they were pretty much all gone. So I picked up the telephone and called the one number I thought I'd never have to call. I, Camille McPhee, dialed 911.

CHAPTER 11

NO EXCUSES

I was waiting in the driveway when Officer Peacock rolled up in his squad car. He wasn't flashing his lights, which was a big surprise to me, because this was a huge emergency. It was below zero. Dustin could get frostbite or hypothermia. If you get frostbite, your fingers, toes, and nose turn black and the doctor has to cut them off. And if you get hypothermia, you get so cold that you go crazy and then you die.

I introduced myself to Officer Peacock as the

babysitter. I told him everything, except the part about Samantha feeding the keys to dogs. I was sure that was against the law. That's when he said, "So your butt was planted in front of the TV when this happened?"

I was really surprised that a police officer would use that kind of language with a ten-year-old. I figured he was one of those people who hated TV and blamed it for everything bad in the world. Clearly, these people weren't aware of the good stations, like CNN, or PBS, or the Game Show Network.

"I bet you got the idea to fix your brother like this from some cop show on TV," he said, wagging his finger at Samantha.

"It was a movie," she whimpered.

"I actually was watching an educational program on the Science Channel," I said.

Officer Peacock stopped in his tracks. He spun around to face me. The sun reflected off his badge and into my eyes, blinding me. When I shaded my eyes with my hand I saw that he had his bolt cutters aimed right at me.

"No excuses!" he huffed. "We got a child chained to a fuel tank and you're the babysitter. No excuses!" He turned back around and stomped through the ankle-high snow into the Bratbergs' backyard toward Dustin and the propane tank.

Dustin was shivering and crying. As Officer Peacock inspected the handcuffs, Dustin pleaded with him to hurry.

"We've got two choices," Officer Peacock said. "First, how important is that hand to you?"

"It's very important to me," he whined. "I write with it."

"I hope I don't have to cut it off."

Dustin fell to his knees, but his arm stayed where it was. The way his arm stretched above him made it look as if he were raising his hand to ask a really important question. I was not happy about this officer's attitude. He was acting like a jerk. I wanted to kick him in the shins and demand that he be nicer to us or I'd kick him again.

But Officer Peacock wasn't the kind of guy you kicked in the shins, even if you had a good reason. He was armed with a gun and a billy club and a terrible personality. He towered over me and Samantha and Dustin in his all-tan uniform. I decided it was best to apologize.

"Normally, I'm the mother's helper," I said. "Being the babysitter is new to me. I'm really sorry about this." I walked over to Dustin and patted him on the back.

"I'm sorry too," Samantha cried, running and throwing her arms around Dustin. "I was a bad sister."

"Back away. Let me use Jaws." Officer Peacock

squeezed the bolt cutters around the cuffs and snapped them off.

Dustin hugged his leg.

"I'll never do this again," he said. "And I'll always look both ways before I cross the street. And I'll never throw candy bar wrappers out the window again. And I won't glue quarters to sidewalks. And I won't toilet-paper supertall trees or stick plastic forks in old people's yards. And when a light turns yellow and my dad asks if he should punch it, I'll tell him no. And—"

"You're welcome," Officer Peacock said, patting Dustin firmly on the back. "You need to stay out of trouble, or those handcuffs will have just been a practice session."

I thought that was an awful thing for Officer Peacock to say. As he drove out of sight, I hooked one arm around Samantha and the other around Dustin and led them back inside. On the Science Channel, two paleontologists were digging up dinosaur bones. I've always felt sorry for dinosaurs. It's never seemed fair to me that such neat-looking animals went extinct.

"This is gross," Dustin said.

Both he and his sister collapsed onto the giant beanbag and continued to watch the TV like zombies. The blue light bounced off their faces, making them look half dead. (Nobody looks attractive when they're watching TV.)

When Mrs. Bratberg came home, I told her what had happened. She apologized several times. Then she took a plastic spatula out of a kitchen drawer and started whipping up a batch of brownies. She told Samantha and Dustin they didn't deserve any. But she said she'd call me when they were done and I could have one. Then I presented her with my sock filled with quarters.

"I don't have time for a math lesson right now," she said.

"Oh," I said.

"How much is in there?" she asked.

"Forty-nine dollars and fifty cents," I said. I would have felt better if it had been fifty dollars, but I had to be honest.

"Let's round up," she said.

I liked that idea.

"Here is seventy dollars. Fifty for your sock. And twenty for your day."

"Thank you so much!" I said.

"Don't spend it all in one place," she said.

This made me frown. Because I only planned on buying one calling card. I slipped the money into the palm of my hand and slid it into my glove.

"Would you like to stay for some pasta salad?" Mrs. Bratberg asked. She opened the refrigerator. "It has sausage and broccoli and eggplant in it."

"I can't," I said. "But I'll save room for a brownie."

I was out of there. My mind zoomed as I walked home. How much would it cost to call Japan? On TV they had commercials for psychics and it cost about five dollars a minute to talk to one of those women and learn about your future. Sally wasn't going to tell me about my future. We'd talk about the past and the present. My call had to be a lot cheaper. Probably a dollar each minute. I figured I'd need thirty more dollars, so we could talk for one hundred minutes, so we could remember each other one hundred percent.

CHAPTER 12

10AD it UP

During the last week of April, spring showed up out of nowhere. The snow melted early. Yellow and purple wildflowers along the road bloomed. The yard turned green again. And I didn't have to wear a jacket anymore. Also, I had saved ten more dollars for my international calling card and had avoided making any friends. I was reminded of how important this was again when Emily Santa, a sixth grader, moved to Guam.

Emily visited our class and gave a report on Guam before she left. At first, she made it sound like a fantastic island and I thought I'd like to visit it one day. But then she started talking about these brown tree snakes that had eaten every single bird on Guam. She made the snakes sound like dangerous criminals. She said that special police were hired to walk around the airport to make sure none of the snakes snuck on a plane and flew to some other island and ruined it. Apparently, Hawaii was really freaked out about this because they have a ton of birds and they aren't that far away from Guam.

But I didn't have to worry about Guam or tree snakes or friends. I remember waking up and hearing birds chirping outside my window and thinking it was some sort of sign. From now on, my life was going to be one big, happy birdsong. Who knew that a trip to the Grand Teton Mall could sink me.

Up to this point, my mother had been a pretty good tightwad. My father said we were finally out of the hole. To help us stay out, my mother carried around a little notebook and scribbled in it every time she made a purchase. She kept track of how much money she spent down to the penny. Personally, I didn't enjoy thinking about the hole.

But that day, my mom's Chevy was almost out of gas, so we drove my dad's pickup to town. I thought we were going grocery shopping. But instead, my mother drove us to the mall. She parked the pickup in the mall's parking lot in front of Macy's and slammed her door much harder than she needed to. Like she was mad at it. Then, walking toward the store, she pulled her little notebook out of her purse and stared at it like it was her enemy. She even growled at it. Then she tried to rip it in half, but it was too thick.

"I hate this thing!" she yelled. She tossed the little book into a bush beside the store.

"But we're finally out of the hole," I said.

It didn't matter. My mother had snapped. And once inside, I snapped too. Worrying about the hole isn't as much fun as shopping.

I'd hoped to go through life as a problem solver. But in this situation, I became a problem maker. I found a fabulous purchase!

I spotted my future mattress in the corner of the Bare Maple Furniture and Mattress Store. It was on display, sheetless and without pillows. I imagined myself curled up on top of it, flipping from my right side to my left, breaking in the new springs, having delightful dreams. Without any squeaking. "This is perfect," I told my mother, stroking it like it was a friendly dog. "It doesn't squeak and it matches the new carpet."

My mother agreed.

"And squeaking isn't good," she said.

"I know. I've been having some pretty weird dreams lately," I said.

"Nothing is more important than a good night's sleep," she said. "Plus, it's on sale. You don't mind sleeping on the display model, do you?"

I shook my head. I didn't mind at all. A new mattress is a new mattress.

When the salesman loaded it into the pickup, he tipped his ball cap at my mother and tugged at a corner of the plastic wrap, saying, "This here is a suffocation risk. Punch some holes in it before you throw it out."

He spat a brown loogie on the ground and shifted his toothpick from one side of his mouth to the other using his tongue.

"My neighbor threw out a big plastic department-store bag and her little Pomeranian got all caught up in it," he said. "It died."

He tossed the toothpick on the ground and spat another brown loogie. "You'd expect that with a cat, but it takes a lot to kill a dog."

I don't know what this guy had against cats. He yanked on the twine to make sure it was tight and then walked to my mother's window. He pulled his ball cap off by its bill and waved goodbye with it. "Drive safely," he said, thumping on the pickup's side rail as we pulled away. I realize now that driving away was a big mistake.

On our way home, it became obvious to everyone— especially the minivan behind us—that we were about to lose our load. My mother was doing forty miles per hour, making the mattress pull against the orange twine, the wind lifting it up like a giant rectangular wing.

"I can sit in the back and hold it down," I offered.

But my mother refused.

"I'm not your father," she said. "If anything happened, if you fell out, your head would pop open like a cherry tomato."

Rather than have us squish in and ride three across in his small pickup, my father would sometimes let me ride in the back, perched on the wheel well of my choice. He would take the back roads, softly turning the corners home.

As the minivan passed, the driver pressed on her horn, releasing long, complaining honks. Even as she pulled ahead, she continued honking, as if she was trying to warn the rest of Yellowstone Highway about us. I hated it when people were showy like that.

"I get it!" my mother yelled out of her window, her hair swirling around her face as she tapped on the brakes. She pulled over to the side of the road, and we both got out to take a look.

No longer in motion, the mattress looked peaceful. The fabric was a light pink, and even in its giant protective plastic wrap, I could see white flowers blooming on it from head to foot. "I didn't count on this wind," my mother said, standing beside the pickup, tugging at the twine. "What do you think?"

I took a minute to reflect on everything I'd learned in school up to this point. But we hadn't really covered anything like this. I also thought about stuff I'd learned on the Science Channel. But that didn't really help either.

"How about we slow down?" I said loudly.

We climbed back into the truck and drove, straddling the fog line in second gear, all the way home. My mother shook her fist at people who honked and made rude hand gestures. I was surprised that so many unkind people had drivers' licenses. When we rolled up in the driveway, my father was out front, sweeping his weed whacker along the ditch bank. He cut the motor when he saw us and laid the machine down in the grass. He was wearing a badly scuffed pair of cowboy boots. Years of yard work had stained the toes a deep froggy green.

Even from far away—just by the way he was standing—I could tell he was thinking about the hole. I could tell he was on the verge of blowing up.

"How much did that thing cost?" he yelled across the lawn, gesturing to the mattress with his arm.

My mother didn't answer. She climbed into the truck bed and untied the twine. I stayed out of her way as she shoved the mattress onto the driveway. It tumbled out like a potato. She didn't ask my father for help. His face looked red and unhappy.

"Don't mind him," she said, dragging my mattress

toward the house. As my father got closer, my mother kept her back to him, sliding my mattress down the front walk.

I tried to calm my father down by using mental energy. Once on TV, I saw a man who could bend spoons with his mind. I used my mind to try to stamp out my father's anger. I sent him the following message forty-seven times:

You like Camille's mattress. You like Camille's mattress.

But my father's mind was very powerful. I think he actually bounced my message back to me and gave me a headache, which was very unfair because he was a lot bigger than me and had a much larger mind.

"Did you get a box spring, too?" he asked my mother, rocking back on his heels, his hands in his pockets.

"Camille needs a mattress," my mother said, walking backward up the cement steps.

"I thought Camille already had a mattress," he said.

"It squeaks," I said.

My mother reached behind her and opened the screen door. She held it open with her butt. I picked up the mattress's other end and helped her steer it inside. Even though my head was throbbing, I sent my father some more messages.

Camille's mattress was an absolute bargain. Camille's mattress was an absolute bargain.

I thought it might be working, because his face looked pink, not red. My mother and I carried my mattress down the hallway and into my room. The house still smelled like carpet glue. But it also smelled like my mother's spicy meatballs. Sadly, they weren't really meatballs. She made them out of extra-firm tofu.

"Do you have plans for the old one?" my father asked, standing in the doorway.

"I'll throw it out," she said, resting the new mattress against a wall.

Go back outside and whack the weeds. Go back outside and whack the weeds.

"The trash service won't pick that up," he said. The doorframe squeaked as he leaned heavily against it.

"They'll take whatever I put out," she said. She pulled my old mattress off my bed.

I tried one last message. *Forget about the hole! Forget about the hole! Forget about the hole!* But it didn't look like it was working. My father looked totally stuck on the hole. At this point, I threw my mental-energy plan out the window.

"She's right," I said. Hearing my mom mention that reminded me of our new trash program. I thought it would help if I explained it to my dad. "It's a brand-new program. On Take-It-Away Tuesday the trash people will take anything. It's the fourth Tuesday of every month. That's how the Hattens threw their dishwasher away, and that's how Penny Winchester's mom got rid of their broken freezer, and that's how the Bratbergs threw that elk away that they accidentally hit with their station wagon."

My father looked surprised. "I thought those hooligans burned that elk," he said. "I thought that's what that smell was."

"No," I said, throwing my arms up with excitement. "It was Take-It-Away Tuesday." I walked toward him and grabbed his hand. "The smell was all of their rotten potatoes. For some reason, they buried over a hundred pounds of potatoes two years ago. And for some other reason, they decided to dig them all up and burn them."

My father let me hold his hand. "How do you know all this? You don't play with their kids, do you?" he asked, looking down at me.

"No," I said, taking my hand back. "I absolutely avoid them. Except when I'm their mother's helper." After I said this, I wished I could have sucked the words back into my mouth. I had promised my mother many times that I would never tell my father.

Forget I just said that. Forget I just said that. Also, keep forgetting about the hole.

My father looked at my mother and back at me. My mother and I hung our heads.

"She just gives Mrs. Bratberg an extra set of hands," my mom said.

"She's not old enough to watch other people's kids," my father said. "What if somebody hit their head, or choked, or drank poison?"

"I'd call 911," I said, folding my arms across my chest. But I didn't go into the actual time I had called 911. I thought this was going bad enough already.

My father glared at me and motioned with his arm for me to leave my room.

"Maxine, at this rate Camille won't live to be eleven. The Bratberg boys build pipe bombs. I've heard them explode. She can't watch them. Even with Mrs. Bratberg there. I don't trust that situation." He made the sound of an explosion, and when my mother tried to interrupt him, he made the sound again. "No playing, no mother's helper, and we're building a fence."

"A fence costs money."

"A fence would be worth every dime!" my father said. "You don't even know if this mattress is new," he said. "It could be refurbished. There could be kid pee, bedbugs, and deadly bacteria in there."

"Shut up, shut up!" my mother said. "Bare Maple Furniture and Mattress Store doesn't sell that kind of garbage."

I stood in the hallway and covered my ears.

Whether or not we thought it was fair, my father had banned my mother and me from shopping at three places: Boing Boing Toys, because the owner's uncle was a convicted felon; Chuck's Grocery, because they'd been caught selling bad meat; and the Grand Teton Mall, because he thought the way big department stores treated small businesses was almost as bad as organized crime.

"Do you respect anything I say?" he yelled, throwing my door open. My father's face was red again, and when he saw me, I tried to act like I hadn't been listening by inspecting my fingernails.

"Go outside," he said to me.

I turned to go.

"No. You could run into our pipe-bomb-building, elk-dumping, potato-burning neighbors," he roared. "Go wait in the garage." Inside my room, I could see my mother sitting on my new mattress, crying. She pulled at the protective plastic, tearing at it, making holes. I tried to send her some mental messages.

Camille still likes you. Camille still likes you.

I hadn't been in the garage for very long when I heard my father drag something out of the house, load it in his pickup, and back out of the driveway. My mother opened the garage door that led to the kitchen and told me to come inside. I ran to my room. My mother had remade my bed. I pulled back the comforter and sheets and touched my brand-new pink mattress. I outlined some of the white blossoms with my pointer finger.

My mother stood in the doorway, her cheeks stained with mascara. "He took the old one to the dump," she said. "Take-It-Away Tuesday is two weeks away."

I looked at her and smiled. "The tofu balls sure smell good," I lied.

"Yeah," she said. "We should eat."

Even though watching my father blow up had totally killed my appetite, I thought that eating my mother's tofu balls was the right thing to do. I slipped off my shoes and followed her to the kitchen. The carpet felt pretty great under my socked feet. Walking down the hall, I wondered about the size of the hole and whether or not the new carpet and mattress had been worth it.

Up and down. Up and down. That's what life was like for me in fourth grade. And I never knew when the downs were going to show up. I couldn't look at the calender and plan for them like I could the Fourth of July or Valentine's Day. They just arrived. And hit me. Like a spit wad. Or a slaughterball.

CHAPTER 13

MONEY MATTERS

I don't know who invented money, but it was a bad idea. It's just not fair that some people wind up in the hole. After my parents fought about my mattress, they started fighting all the time. It was as if it were the only thing they knew how to do anymore. And when I said, "Keep your domestic problems to yourselves," they kept fighting. And when I said, "You need mediation," they kept fighting. Sometimes louder. Sometimes slamming a door.

After they fought, during the quiet time that followed, either my mother or my father would come and find me.

"I'm sorry I yelled at your father, Camille. I still love you," my mother said.

"Camille, just because I fight with your mother, it doesn't mean I love you any less," my father said.

But I was never worried about how much they loved me. I knew that. I was worried about how much they seemed to hate each other. They should not have said the things they did. "Don't try to manipulate me, Maxine!" said my father.

"If you wanted a tightwad, you should've married a tightwad," said my mother.

It was terrible. And I didn't call Aunt Stella every time this happened. Because I didn't want to make her sad. Because being a nurse all day long was already hard enough. It was a tough time. I tried to bring my dingo strategy home with me. I'd ask myself, *What would a dingo do?* But the truth was, I had no idea. I didn't know much about dingoes, other than what they looked like. And my dad wouldn't buy me a book about dingoes, because the only one we found cost thirty dollars and he said it was too much money.

"They're just dogs," he told me.

But I knew that wasn't true. Because I had not been

acting like a dog at school for the past seven months, I had been acting like a dingo. I hugged the book to my chest and fell to my knees.

"This book would be worth every penny," I said.

But he said, "No way, José. Get up off the floor."

And I got up off the floor. And I didn't say anything else. My dad didn't understand how important dingo information was to me.

During this time, school was pretty terrible too. Science kept getting more and more advanced. I was learning things about pesticides. And the "R factor," which is the resistance a pest has to a pesticide. Finding out about these things made me very frightened of fruits and vegetables that were not organic. I made my mother wash all apples for five minutes before I would touch them. Then, in math we started dividing numbers again. Which seemed like a bad idea.

Plus, Tony Maboney bought a new, huge pencil with an extra-firm eraser, and he never got tired of poking me. And then, when I thought things couldn't get any worse, Ms. Golden gave her gifted reading students some terrible news. One day, before she handed out our books, she told us that she was scheduled for surgery, and that it was very possible that she was going to die. Okay. That's not exactly what she said. Ms. Golden told us that she was going to have her tonsils removed. And that we would be staying in Mr. Hawk's class for reading for an entire week.

"No!" I said.

I didn't mean to say this. It just came out. Ms. Golden smiled at me.

"I'll miss you too. All of you," she said.

And then Penny asked, "But what about the play?"

And I wasn't even sure what Penny was talking about. As far as I knew, our next unit in gifted reading was about folktales. Ms. Golden had already told us all about it. She said she believed it was time that we studied "the vast history of the human past." So we would be reading stories that were written a long time ago in other countries. Like France. And Germany. And Alabama.

"Well, I'm very happy that everybody liked last year's production. But this year, I'm not going to direct the play."

This is when I had a realization. I'd been so busy thinking about the hole, and looking for Checkers, and worrying about my wolverine parents that the fact that elementary schools had school plays and that ours was coming up had totally slipped my mind.

"No school play?" Lilly cried.

"There will be a school play," Ms. Golden said. "But this year there will be a special, new director."

And the way Ms. Golden said the word *special* made me very nervous.

But I kept my concern to myself. That day, we finished our unit on legends. We read a story about a boy named Kana who had amazing stretching abilities and brought the sun and the moon and the stars back to the sky after they were taken by a guy named Kahoaalii who obviously had some sharing issues. It was a pretty good legend. But I didn't think it was as good as Sedna. Because that one had seals in it.

When we got back to Mr. Hawk's classroom, it was time for art. And I loved art. Except sometimes I spilled the glue. Even when we weren't supposed to be using the glue. For some reason, I enjoyed squeezing the glue until it bubbled out of the bottle. Sitting at my desk, I noticed that Mr. Hawk didn't have out any of the tubs with the art supplies in them. What was he waiting for?

Then Mrs. Zirklezack, the Rocky Mountain Elementary School kindergarten teacher, walked into my classroom and stood beside Mr. Hawk's dark wooden desk. She said that she had news about the school play.

Mrs. Zirklezack clapped to get our attention. And when she did that, I thought it was very obvious that she taught kindergarten.

"This year we're going to do a play that I wrote."

I could tell that nobody in the room was excited.

Last year, when Ms. Golden directed the production of *Peter Pan,* we were all very thrilled. Because that play had a lot of good parts. And since we were all third graders, we hadn't gotten to be in it. Because first, second, and third grades do a chorus production, not a school play. This year, even though it wasn't likely, a lot of us were hoping that we would do *Peter Pan* again. That way, those of us who didn't get a chance to be a pirate could have another shot.

"What's your play's name?" Penny asked.

I turned around and looked at Penny. I was impressed that she would ask a kindergarten teacher that without even raising her hand.

"The play is called *Nora Saves the World,*" Mrs. Zirklezack said.

"Does it have space aliens in it?" Tony Maboney asked.

"No," Mrs. Zirklezack said. "*Nora Saves the World* is a play about saving animals."

"This sounds very interesting," Mr. Hawk said.

"Are there penguins in it?" Penny asked.

"Let's let Mrs. Zirklezack finish," Mr. Hawk said.

Mrs. Zirklezack clapped again. She had such a wide smile on her face that she looked a little spooky. I could see her yellow teeth and her bright pink gums and it really surprised me that her husband was an orthodontist. Some of her teeth were pointy like vampire teeth, and if I were married to an orthodontist and had long, yellow, pointy vampire teeth, I'd have them fixed. Even if it meant that I had to have my teeth filed down. Or yanked out.

"This is a story about salvation," Mrs. Zirklezack said. "And yes, there are penguins in it. And there are camels. And gorillas. And crocodiles. And parrots. And giraffes. And lots of other animals."

People seated around me seemed excited to learn this.

"How does Nora save the world?" Penny asked.

Mr. Hawk frowned at Penny. He disapproved of all her interrupting.

"Great question," Mrs. Zirklezack said. "Nora lives in a world that is half sunny and half rainy. Everything is fine for a long time. But eventually, all the factories make the sunny days end. And every day becomes rainy."

"Is your play about global warming?" Penny asked.

"Shhh," Mr. Hawk said.

"The play is about personal strength," Mrs. Zirklezack said. "When Nora realizes that the rain won't stop, she decides to save all the animals of the world. After many challenging rescues, she gathers them all up in her bus. And they drive away to a sunny, safe place. I'm leaving a list of all your parts at the front of the room. Sixth graders run the factories. And fifth and fourth graders will be the animals. We start practice next week."

When Mrs. Zirklezack opened her arms wide, I saw little fat pockets jiggle. Because my mother taught aerobics, she had explained every boring muscle to me. So I knew that Mrs. Zirklezack needed to tone her triceps. I also knew that this was considered a "problem area" for a lot of women. She waved to us and we waved back. And then she walked away. After she left, Mr. Hawk brought out the art tubs.

"We'll be doing free drawing today," Mr. Hawk said.

This was a huge relief. Because it meant I could let my mind and hands do whatever they wanted.

"I want to be a penguin," Penny said, rushing toward the list.

"I hope I'm a crocodile," Tony Maboney said.

"I wonder who will be cast as Nora?" Lilly asked.

I didn't care about that. The last thing in the world I'd want to be was Nora. In fact, I thought the whole play sounded pretty bad. I didn't understand how the bus could drive to safety if the whole world was being rained on. Were there places that didn't have factories that were still okay? Or was Nora planning to drive to a high elevation in the mountains? Wouldn't there be an

121

awful lot of snow there? And how would Nora fit all these animals onto a single bus? And wouldn't the tigers eat all the other animals? And also Nora?

As I looked over the list, I stopped worrying about tigers and started worrying about something else. I didn't see my name. I read the list again. It was big. When you added up fourth, fifth, and sixth grades, there were about eighty of us. Twenty were the sixth-grade factory workers, so I didn't have to look at those parts. I read through the animals. There were thirty different kinds that Nora saved. Two of each. Penny was a sea lion. Lilly was a dolphin. Tony Maboney was a turtle. Polly was a parrot. But I didn't see my name anywhere. I wondered if maybe Mrs. Zirklezack had heard about me falling underneath my school bus and worried that I'd somehow mess up her bus play. So she kept me out.

I read the list over and over. But it wasn't like I could make my name appear. Finally, I walked away. I guess I didn't need a part. I could just sit in the audience and watch Nora pack those animals onto her bus.

I decided that drawing a blue butterfly was the only way to cheer myself up. Digging through the art tubs for an appropriate number of colored pencils, I accidentally scratched Polly's hand.

"Ouch," she said.

"Sorry," I said.

"That's okay," she said. "My cat scratches me all the time. Accidents happen."

"I guess," I said.

"I'm a parrot," Polly said. "What are you?"

I shrugged.

"I didn't see your name on the list," Polly said.

I shrugged again.

"It's probably a mistake. Maybe you should talk to Mr. Hawk."

I took my hands out of that tub and put them in the one next to it. And I quit talking to Polly. Because I didn't need her telling me how to solve my problems. I didn't need her telling me anything.

CHAPTER 14

TAKING A BREAK

When I came home from school, partless and carrying a picture of an extremely blue butterfly, my parents didn't even notice that I was upset. Even when I said, "I sure am feeling upset."

They were at it again. My mother had bought a pot rack for the kitchen. Apparently, pot racks are really expensive, and buying one puts you deeper in the hole. When my dad came home, he walked right into it, banging his head against several pans.

"Every penny you have burns a hole in your pocket," he said.

"If I had enough cupboard space, I wouldn't need a pot rack," my mother said.

"You'll never have enough of anything," he said. "I've seen the way you grocery shop. You'll load anything into the cart. Anything!"

"I buy what we need!" she said. "Sometimes I even use coupons."

"Maxine, at the rate you spend money, we'll never make it back out of the hole!"

I thought my dad made some good points. But it would have been better if he hadn't said them so loudly, or maybe he could have softened them by phrasing them in the form of a question.

"So what if we're in the hole!" my mother said.

"Are you kidding me? When we're in the hole, we're always juggling bills and we can't enjoy life," my dad said.

"What's so bad about juggling bills?" my mom asked.

"It's too stressful. Our mortgage payment sits on top of me like an actual house. When you spend and spend, I feel like I have to work more and more," my dad said.

I walked to my bedroom and shut the door. I even put my head under my pillows. But I could still hear them. I hated it when they talked about our mortgage payment.

"Maybe you *should* work more," my mother said.

"Maybe I will," my father said.

"I need a break from this!" my mother said.

I threw the pillow off my head and sat up. I couldn't believe my mother was saying this. Married people don't take breaks. She knew that. You're either married, separated, or divorced. Was she asking for a separation? By now, I was breathing very quickly. But I wasn't overly worried, because I knew that my dad was a levelheaded and fair-minded person. He would smooth things out.

"A break sounds fantastic!" he said. "I've got a trip planned to Seattle and Portland. I'll tack on Alaska and be gone four weeks. How does that sound?"

I pulled open my door and ran out into the hall. Four weeks? He'd never been gone that long before. Two weeks was the limit. Had he forgotten that? Everything felt wrong. Instead of saying what he was supposed to say, he was saying crazy things. I mean, four weeks? He should have said, "Let's calm down and talk about this. I love you. I love Camille. We don't need to take a break. It's dollar cone day at the Yogurt Shack. Let's go get some." Then everyone was supposed to hug. This was all wrong!

My father lugged an enormous brown suitcase out of the closet. I went into my parents' bedroom and watched him jerk open drawers. He gathered clothes and stuffed them inside the suitcase. Seeing his underwear and socks piled up in there made me very sad.

"You don't need this!" I said, trying to throw his clothes back out of the suitcase. "Just go for two weeks. Or don't go at all."

"I need to go," he said.

"Then stick to the limit and come back after two weeks," I said. "Please."

"I don't think that will be long enough," he said.

"But maybe you can still fix things."

But my father shook his head.

"Fix things!" I cried.

He zipped the suitcase closed.

I didn't know what else to do. My father walked over to me and kissed the top of my head.

"I love you, Camille. But your mother's right. We both need a break."

I knew he was planning to go away again. But not like this. Not when he was angry. Not for a whole month!

"Maybe you need to talk to somebody. What about mediation?" I asked. "You should contact Mrs. Moses. She's great."

But my father kept walking away.

"I don't think your vice principal can help us," he said. "Maybe when I come back, we can sit down and talk to somebody."

"Let's talk to somebody now," I said.

My father shook his head.

"I need to get on the road," he said.

As my father pulled his suitcase out to his pickup, I stood at the living room window and watched. I could feel my heart beating deep inside of me.

My mother came up behind me and stroked my hair.

"I hate this," I told her. "Why does it have to be like this? Is it that hard to stay out of the hole?"

My mother turned me around and kissed my forehead.

"I'm sorry," she said. "I'm doing the best that I can. But I am what I am."

That night, when she tucked me into bed, it was very hard for me to keep my tears from flooding out of my eyes.

"Don't cry, sweetheart," my mother said. "I love you."

"I know that," I said. "I just wish life had more ups and less downs."

"Yeah," she said. "That would be nice."

I sniffled hard and she got me some tissues.

"Is there anything else you want to talk about?" my mother asked.

I shook my head.

"You haven't talked about school lately," she said.

"It's pretty much the same," I said.

"What are you learning about in science?" she asked.

"Cells," I said.

"What about cells?" she asked.

"We're studying the structural difference between plant and animal cells," I said.

"That sounds extremely advanced for fourth grade," she said.

"I guess," I said.

"What about math?"

"We're dividing stuff," I said.

"Do you still play slaughterball in PE?" she asked.

I nodded. "And the janitor recently reinflated all the balls, so now they're extra bouncy and hard."

"I'm so sorry," she said.

"Yeah. Me too," I said.

And even though my mother kissed me goodnight and told me to sleep well, I didn't sleep well that whole night. I flipped and flopped. And every time my mattress didn't squeak, it made me think of the hole. So I tried to stay very still, as stiff as a bone, so I could fall asleep. But even when I did that, my mind kept moving around.

Why would my mother say that she wanted my father to leave? Did she really want that? That's not what I wanted. I wanted my whole family to continue to live in my house with me. And how could my father pack his suitcase and drive away like that? Driving away means giving up. Was that what he wanted to do? Why would my father want to do that?

CHAPTER 15

SYMBOLISM

In the den, my mother punched the air and released angry grunts. I'd never seen her jab anything with that much force before. She saw me watching her and winked.

"I packed an extra piece of cheese in your cooler," she said.

An extra piece of cheese? Did she think that would fix how I felt? Had she forgotten about the terrible thing that had happened last night? Because I sure hadn't. In fact, it felt like it was still happening.

I got ready for school as fast as I could. Because I was trying to free up five spare minutes. I wanted to make an important phone call. I needed to talk to Aunt Stella immediately. Aunt Stella was the only person I could think of on the planet (who didn't live in Japan) who could make me feel better. When my mom began practicing her "ball work," I decided that would be the perfect time. But it wasn't. Because I got Aunt Stella's voice mail and I had to leave my message at the sound of the beep.

"Aunt Stella. It's Camille. Things are very terrible here. Have you ever heard of a pot rack? Mom bought one. And Dad blew up. And now they're separated. And Dad packed a suitcase with eight pairs of underwear in it. And sometimes he washes those in the sink in his hotel. So he could be gone a lot longer than eight days. He said he's going away for four weeks. And Mom seems fine about the whole thing. But I'm not. I'm sad. And now I've got to go to school."

Even with my extra piece of cheese, I was so sad when I went out to catch the bus, I almost forgot I was a dingo. Polly was wearing a pair of checkered green pants that were really cute, and I almost told her that I liked them. But I didn't.

"Don't fall!" Danny yelled as I crossed the road to board the bus.

"Roadkill McPhee," Manny hollered.

I kept my head down. *Dingo. Dingo. Dingo.*

"Don't listen to them," Polly said. "I like your shirt," she added.

I noticed that Polly was wearing a shirt that said I LOVE MY CAT. I thought it was so tacky that it made her pants look less cute. But I didn't say anything. Polly sat next to me and smiled several times. I focused on looking at my own hands.

"Hey, is that your mom?" Polly asked, pointing out the window.

"I think so," I said.

I watched my mother's blue Chevy pass the bus. The bus was higher than the other traffic, so I could see inside her car. She was wearing a long coat over her pink aerobics clothes.

"She's in a hurry," Polly said.

I shrugged.

It made me sad to see my mother zoom by me. She was so close to my school that I thought she should have offered to drive me there and drop me off. It was the "Mom thing" to do. Then I got very nervous. Maybe now that my dad had left, my mom was going to stop doing "Mom things."

When we got to school, I did my best to get away

from Polly and sit down at my desk. But I couldn't. Because the door to our classroom was shut.

"Somebody's mom is in there," Tony Maboney said.

I nodded and stood in line behind Lilly.

"It looks like your mom," Polly said.

I stood on my tiptoes and looked through the door's window. It was my mother in there. She was talking to Mr. Hawk and flapping her arms around. What was she doing? I didn't know. I couldn't hear what she was saying.

"She looks wet," Penny said. "Wait, I think she's sweating."

My eyes got very huge. I didn't like the idea of my mom sweating next to my teacher in my classroom. She should sweat in the den at home. Or the aerobics room at the gym. And that was it.

Penny crammed her face right up into the window. "She's wearing a bandana. And wristbands."

Lilly peeked too. "Is your mom an aerobics instructor?" she asked me.

I nodded. But I felt so terrible that I wished I could have melted into my shoes and become invisible. Just before the bell rang, my mother walked out of my classroom. Her coat fluttered open and I could see her pink top and pink shorts. I closed my eyes. Then I felt her warmth as she leaned toward me and kissed the top of my head.

"It's taken care of," she said.

When I opened my eyes she was gone. Everybody walked into the classroom. I thought people would tease me and make fun of my mom and her pink clothes. But they didn't.

"I think your mom teaches my mom's favorite class," Lilly said. "My mom loves it!"

"Oh," I said.

"Does you mom teach kickboxing?" Penny asked. "I think my mom takes her class too."

"Yes," I said. "She also does a lot of ball work."

And then everybody started taking about how cool kickboxing was. Because it was exercise, but it was also a way to defend yourself if you got mugged. And I acted like I thought it was cool too. Even though I thought sweating was pretty uncool. Then the bell rang, and Mr. Hawk said he had some news for us.

"When you look up, I'm sure you can see one of my all-time favorite assignments."

We all looked up. And I stared at that cricket. And, for the first time, I noticed that it had a very pointy butt. It was a good thing that I was going to get rid of it.

"That's right," he said. "Constructing arthropods."

For the first time in a long time, I felt a little bit excited, because this was the assignment I'd been waiting for all year.

"As some of you may or may not know, modern

arthropods include insects, spiders, centipedes, shrimp, and crayfish," he said.

I felt my spirits lifting higher and higher. Because I knew that a butterfly was an insect. And so I could build one of those for my arthropod.

"Traditionally, I ask my students to assemble their arthropods using affordable craft items from home."

Which meant I could use blue material, and glitter, and pipe cleaners, and beads, and yarn, and feathers, and sponges, and toothpaste, and anything else I wanted. I licked my lips.

"But it's been brought to my attention that some of my assignments have been too similar to what I assigned to my sixth-grade students," Mr. Hawk said.

Uh-oh. I wondered if that was why my mother was here.

"I believe in challenging my classes," he said. "But based on a recent conversation, I'm beginning to think that the arthropod assignment might be a little too advanced."

I lowered my head and looked at the floor.

"Instead of building arthropods, I'm going to assign a project that's related to solar power. For the first part of the assignment, I'd like you to all go home today and count how many lightbulbs you have in your house. Any questions?"

I looked around the room. Was everybody okay

with this? I mean, we weren't going to be building arthropods. That wasn't fair. Because all year long I'd put up with a hornet dangling above me. And then a cricket. And the reason I did this was because I had hope that there would eventually be a butterfly up there. But now Mr. Hawk was telling me that there was no hope. And that I had to count lightbulbs. I put my head down on my desk.

"Do porch lights count?" Penny asked.

"Yes," Mr. Hawk said.

"Do fish-tank lights count?" Boone Berry asked.

"Yes," Mr. Hawk said.

"What about the motion-detector security light that's attached to my garage?" Nina asked.

"Absolutely," Mr. Hawk said.

"Does the light in the refrigerator count?" Lilly asked. "Because most of the time, it's not even on."

"Yes, the lightbulb in your refrigerator counts," Mr. Hawk said. "Any lightbulb you find, you should count."

I lifted my head up and opened my desk so I could peek inside it. I'd already started collecting stuff to build my butterfly. A blue shoelace. Sparkly paper. Blue sticky tape. Now none of those things mattered. Those things were as useful as garbage. Which didn't have any use. All garbage was good for was spreading bugs and disease. I closed my desk and tried not to look up at the cricket.

"All right, Mrs. Zirklezack is having play practice in the gym this afternoon. But she's dropped off the scripts for us to read through. It's a very interesting story."

I wasn't very excited to read *Nora Saves the World*. But I took a copy of the script anyway. Mr. Hawk had everybody take turns reading it aloud. We read about Nora, a bus driver, who realized that if it rained every day, soon all the animals in the zoo would drown. Nobody who ran the factories would listen to her. They all had huge egos and didn't care about the size of their carbon footprints. Not a single one of them loved the earth. So one day, Nora took her bus and loaded it with hay and provisions and rescued all the animals. Some of them, like the gorillas, didn't want to come, and she had to trick them onto the bus by tempting them with bananas. In the end, Nora and the whole bus drove to a sunny spot. And they disembarked. And planted an amazing garden. And celebrated never needing another factory. And they lived happily ever after.

"Pretty good story," Mr. Hawk said, after we finished reading it.

"Wait a minute," Penny said. "There's a lot of things that don't make sense."

"It's a story," Mr. Hawk said. "You're supposed to suspend your sense of disbelief a little."

"But if I'm a sea lion, why do I care if the world floods? I can swim," Penny said.

"Good point," Lilly said. "I'm a dolphin. I shouldn't be stuck on a bus with hay. I'll die!"

"This play feels like it was written for kindergarten kids," Penny said. "It's not even believable. I mean, in addition to everything we've already pointed out, Nora doesn't save a single bear."

"Yeah!" Tony Maboney said.

And at that point, we all decided as a class that Mrs. Zirklezack's play was rotten.

"We should do *Peter Pan* again," Jory said.

"Yeah!" Tony Maboney yelled. "I want to play Captain Hook!"

"Stop yelling," Mr. Hawk said. "Everybody needs to take five deep breaths."

I listened to my class suck in air and blow it out. We did this five times. Then I saw Polly raise her hand.

"I have a problem with the play too," Polly said.

"Let's try to stay positive," Mr. Hawk said.

And so Polly never got the chance to say what her problem was.

After lunch, Mr. Hawk's class gathered in the auditorium. Because Mrs. Zirklezack had forgotten that I existed, I hadn't been assigned a role yet. So I just tried to blend in with the students who were animals. It seemed like everyone else had a place to be. During practice, I felt left out, especially when I stood near the zebras. They were pretty snooty. Mrs. Zirklezack explained where everybody was supposed to stand. And she put masking tape on the floor so that we wouldn't forget our spots.

"You're all doing such a good job!" she cheered. It took over an hour, but we went through the whole entire play.

"Does anybody have any questions?" Mrs. Zirklezack asked.

"Yeah," Penny said. "Why are the sea lions and dolphins being forced onto a bus?"

I looked at Mrs. Zirklezack to see what her reaction would be.

"It's symbolic," she said.

"But they'd die," Penny said. "I thought this play was about saving things."

"Again, it's symbolic," Mrs. Zirklezack said.

Penny shook her head. She looked pretty mad about being a sea lion. And Lilly looked pretty disappointed about being a dolphin, too.

"I'd prefer to swim alongside the bus," Lilly said.

"Oh no," Mrs. Zirklezack said. "In the final scene, all the animals disembark from the bus together. It's a very important moment."

Penny rolled her eyes.

"Any other questions?" Mrs. Zirklezack asked.

Polly raised her hand. This surprised me. Because

she usually didn't raise her hand except when she had to go to the bathroom.

"Camille doesn't have a part. She hasn't been assigned anything," Polly said.

Mrs. Zirklezack studied her clipboard. "What's your last name, Camille?"

Everybody looked at me and I began breathing very quickly.

"McPhee," I said.

"Camille McPhee," Mrs. Zirklezack said. "Well, this is a problem."

I didn't like being thought of as a problem.

"But every problem has a solution. I'll figure something out," Mrs. Zirklezack said. "Now, everybody go back to class."

We walked back to class in a big clump, our shoes squeaking across the gymnasium floor. Penny and Lilly wouldn't stop talking about how much they hated their parts.

"I'll look like a joke," Penny said. "Everybody is going to laugh at me."

"Me too," Lilly said. "It's not fair."

And when Penny said that, I almost jumped right into her conversation and said, "That's right. Life isn't fair." But I didn't do that. I just kept walking. In the end, I didn't think being a symbolic sea lion or dolphin was as bad as they made it sound. At least they both had parts.

CHAPTER 16

talk it Out

When I got home, I didn't even look for my mother. I grabbed the phone and tried to call Aunt Stella. I dialed her number so fast that I accidentally called a dry cleaner.

"Sorry!" I said.

Next time, I dialed more carefully.

"Camille, I got your message," Aunt Stella said.

"Isn't it the worst news ever?" I asked.

"It's pretty bad," she said.

"What am I supposed to do?" I asked. "Dad can't stay gone for four weeks. He can't!"

There was a little bit of silence.

"Aunt Stella?" I asked.

"Camille, I'm going to tell you something and it's not pretty," Aunt Stella said.

"I'm ready," I said. But that was a lie. I was not ready to hear anything ugly.

"These are your parents' problems. And there's absolutely nothing you can do," Aunt Stella said.

I started to cry.

"I wish I could fix this," Aunt Stella said.

"It's because we're in the hole," I said.

"Well, that's part of it," Aunt Stella said. "But sometimes married people hit rocky times."

"I know. I know," I said. "They have ups and downs."

"That's very perceptive," Aunt Stella said. "Camille, I love you so much. Is there anything I can do to make you feel better?"

But I couldn't think of anything.

"I just like talking to you," I said.

"You can call me any time," Aunt Stella said.

"You're not worried about our phone bill?" I asked.

"I'm more concerned about you," she said.

And I thought that was one of the nicest things anybody had ever told me.

"What's going on at school?" she asked.

And I didn't even know how to start to answer that

question. Because way too many things were going on at school. So I just said the first thing that popped into my mind.

"I miss my friend Sally," I said.

"The girl who moved to Japan?" Aunt Stella asked.

"Uh-huh," I said.

"Well, parents tend to move most when their kids are still in grade school. But once they start junior high, it's usually a different story," Aunt Stella said.

"What?" I asked.

"In my experience, parents tend to move around more when their kids are younger. Once they get into the upper-grade levels, it's more likely they'll stay put," Aunt Stella said.

"How come I've never heard this?" I asked. Nobody had ever mentioned that rule before. I didn't know I wasn't supposed to make friends until I was in junior high. This was useful information. Because I didn't know whether or not I was prepared to be a dingo for that long.

"I'm sorry you miss Sally," Aunt Stella said.

"Moving ruins everything," I said.

"You'll make other friends, Camille. You're very charming!" Aunt Stella said.

But I didn't even care if people found me charming or not. Because if my friends might move at any moment, I decided it was better to wait until they were in junior high and would stay put before I became friends with them.

"I better go," I said. "We've been talking for a lot of minutes."

"Camille, I'm going to call you tomorrow. Okay?"

I nodded.

"Are you still there, Camille?" Aunt Stella asked.

"Yes," I said. "I'll talk to you tomorrow."

After I hung up the phone, I went in search of jelly beans. Because those things always made me feel better—for about five minutes. And then I began to feel worse. After I'd shoved quite a few into my mouth, my mother came into my room.

"What are you eating?" she asked.

And I knew that I wasn't supposed to eat jelly beans, so I didn't exactly say that I was eating them.

"Fruit flavors," I said.

"What do you mean, you're eating fruit flavors?" my mother asked.

"I'm eating the flavors cherry and lime and blueberry and piña colada," I said. Then I wished I hadn't said that last flavor.

"Piña colada?" my mother asked. Then she gasped. "Are you eating candy?"

I bit my lip.

"Camille! Do you understand how bad simple sugars are for your system?"

I nodded. Even though I understood that, simple sugars still tasted very good.

"Your blood sugar will spike and then you'll crash!" she said.

The words *spike* and *crash* always frightened me.

"Don't worry. I've only eaten about twenty," I said.

My mother brought her hand to her mouth and gasped again.

"Get in the kitchen right now! You need to eat some cottage cheese!" she said.

So I did.

While I was spooning cottage cheese into my mouth, my mother came out of my bedroom holding a medium-size bag of jelly beans. They looked delicious.

"Where did you get these?" she asked.

But that was a hard question. Because I got them from lots of places. Sally had bought me a couple of bags before she moved. My father had brought me home some from Pleasant Prairie, Wisconsin, because there is a jelly bean factory there. And I'd been given a whole bunch at school from my Secret Santa. And I even bought some myself with my own money.

"How did you accumulate this many beans?" my mother asked.

She shook the bag in front of me and it made the beans shake in a very yummy way.

"I've been saving them for a long time," I said. "And I eat them responsibly."

"Twenty!" she said.

Then she set the beans down on the counter. And walked over to me and my cottage cheese.

"Camille, you can't eat candy. It's not good for you. It will make your blood sugar go up very high and then crash very low. You'll get a headache and feel miserable. Do you understand?"

I shoved a whole bunch of cottage cheese in my mouth and let it sit on my tongue. She went over and picked the bag back up.

"If I didn't love you, I'd give you back your bag of jelly beans and let you eat them all," she said.

Then I watched her take the lid off the trash can and dump in my jelly beans. Even after she stopped pouring them, I could hear the beans rattling their way to the bottom.

"Doesn't that feel better?" she asked.

"Not really," I said.

"Trust me," she said. "It will."

She came and sat down next to me and rubbed my back.

"Do you have any homework?" she asked.

"Math," I said.

She smiled big.

"No *advanced* science?" she asked.

I shook my head.

"A little bird told me that science is going to become much less advanced," she said. "Also, no more slaughterball."

She kissed my head and then got up and started flapping her arms like they were wings.

"That's okay, honey. You don't have to thank me."

CHAPTER 17

CAT FATE

I really missed gifted reading. Because not only did I miss reading, but I also missed sitting in a bean-bag chair. Mostly, I missed Ms. Golden. So when Mr. Hawk said he had some bad news about Ms. Golden, I thought I was going to start crying in front of everybody.

"Ms. Golden will be out for another week," Mr. Hawk said.

"Was there a problem with her surgery?" Penny asked. "Did they take out the wrong tonsil?"

I thought that was a pretty good question.

"No," Mr. Hawk said. "She's just taking an extra week to recuperate."

He sat down at his desk and smiled.

"But I've got some good news," he said. "Mrs. Zirklezack has tweaked her play to accommodate some of our class's feedback. Also, she assigned the final part."

Polly turned around and smiled at me. But I didn't smile back. Because I wasn't sure how I felt about this.

When we went to play practice, and Mrs. Zirklezack walked into the gym and smiled one of her spookiest smiles ever, I knew right away that I wasn't going to like my part.

Mrs. Zirklezack called out a list of seven names. They were all girls, and my name was the last one. Penny Winchester, Gracie Clop, Nina Hosack, Lilly Poe, Zoey Combs, Hannah Pond, Camille McPhee.

"When I assigned the final part, I noticed that we had an odd number of animals. That didn't work. So I changed some things. I've decided to make a chorus line," she said, clapping. "You're going to have your own musical number. You're going to be cats."

Lilly squealed.

"Does this mean I'm not a sea lion anymore?" Penny asked.

"That's right," Mrs. Zirklezack said. "I've decided

to omit all references to aquatic animals. In the end, I thought it was a good idea not to load them onto the bus."

"So I'm not a dolphin?" Lilly asked.

"Correct. You're all cats," Mrs. Zirklezack said. And while all the other cats started gabbing about how excited they were about their parts, Mrs. Zirklezack began explaining the cats' "function."

"Look around," she said. And so we did. "No, I'm not talking about the Rocky Mountain Elementary School gymnasium. I'm talking about the civilized world. The cat population is out of control. I want our play to confront this issue head-on."

Mrs. Zirklezack began distributing new scripts. We all flipped through them to see what our parts looked like.

"Oh my heck!" yelled Jasmine Rey, the amazingly popular sixth grader who'd been given the part of Nora. "You're all going to die!"

I flipped through my script until I found the page. It was true. While all the other animals boarded the bus and headed to the sunny, safe place, the cats didn't join them. There wasn't room. Also, when Nora tried to catch us, we ran away.

"I want the audience to be reminded of how tragically overpopulated our communities are with unwanted cats," Mrs. Zirklezack said.

We were supposed to sing a song called "We Can't Come, We Won't Come." Mrs. Zirklezack wrote it herself. The song started off talking about how we wished there were more room for us. But then the song ends with all the cats deciding to just play around.

"This is depressing," Penny said.

"No," Mrs. Zirklezack corrected. "You're not depressed cats. You're a group of sassy cats. You're going to be happy, willful, dancing little beasts. Nora tries to catch you, but you're so busy singing and dancing that you get left behind."

"I thought there wasn't room for us," Lilly said. "I thought that's why we got left."

"That's part of the problem," Mrs. Zirklezack said. "But you're also very sassy."

When Mrs. Zirklezack talked, she opened her arms out wide, and the little pockets of fat under her arms kept jiggling.

"You'll be performing on top of these white plastic buckets," she said, holding a bucket above her head so that we could all see it.

"Why?" Penny asked.

"It heightens the visual drama," Mrs. Zirklezack said. "Plus, everybody will be able to see you."

At first, I thought this was horrible, because if I tipped off my bucket, I knew that I would always be labeled as the hypoglycemic kid who kept falling down.

That was a lot of pressure. But then I realized it might be a good opportunity to show everybody that falling under the school bus was a onetime sort of thing. I could change my reputation.

I took my assigned bucket and looked around. By the deflated expressions on the other cats' faces, it was clear they were disappointed with their roles.

"We're going to die too early," Penny mumbled.

"And too quickly," Lilly added.

When Mrs. Zirklezack handed Penny her bucket, Penny blurted out how she felt.

"Real cats would try to live," she said. "They'd scamper up trees or something."

I looked around at the other cats. A lot of us were smiling. Everybody liked Penny's idea. We didn't want to think of ourselves as disposable cats.

"But your deaths are symbolic," Mrs. Zirklezack said. "You're struck down while misbehaving." Her eyes twinkled when she said this and I thought someone would present her with the idea that we actually should be struck down by lightning or the hand of God, but no one did, and I didn't bring it up.

After practice Polly came up to me and smiled. Her hair was looking less and less stringy these days, but I didn't know why. Maybe she'd started using a volumizing shampoo. I should have told her that her hair looked good.

"You've finally got a part." She beamed. She was carrying a big, bright red and yellow parrot head on a stick. I was surprised by how great some of the animal costumes looked already.

"Yeah," I mumbled.

"Cats are great! And you get to sing and dance!"

"I guess," I said, shrugging. "Until I drown."

When we got back to Mr. Hawk's class, we didn't have time to talk about lightbulbs.

"Tomorrow," he said. "Don't forget your spelling homework. Or your health worksheets. And remember that we're in the computer lab first thing in the morning. So don't show up with sticky fingers. We want to leave the keyboards the way we found them."

CHAPTER 18

DOUBLE-CHECKING

When I got home, my mom wasn't there. She'd left a messy note that was hard to read.

I punctured my inflatable ball on a shoe!
I went to buy another ball! Be back soon!

Underneath it she'd scribbled: "I bet I'm back before you read this note!" But she wasn't.

My mother had recently purchased several pairs of dangerous high-heeled shoes. It didn't surprise me too much that she could pop her ball with one of them. One thing I'd learned already in life was that anything was possible. I walked into my bedroom and opened up my jelly bean drawer. (That's also where I kept my socks.) And I did some double-checking for a runaway bean. But there weren't any. They were all in the garbage can. So I went to the kitchen and lifted the lid off the garbage can and tried to look all the way to the bottom. But it stank so bad that I had to put the lid back on. Also, I gagged a little.

As I walked back to my bedroom, I heard the answering machine going *beep, beep, beep*. I tried to ignore that sound and got out my spelling homework. This week was a hard list: *void, point, trapezoid, poison, moist, ointment, destroy, royal,* and *oyster*. And our bonus word was *employee*. The reason we were studying these words was because we were learning about diphthongs. That's when two vowels join together to make one sound.

My mother came home carrying three bags. I looked up, but then I went back to work.

"I thought I'd beat you home," she said.

"You didn't," I said.

"Don't you want to know what I bought?" she asked.

I shook my head.

"Camille, you'll find this very interesting!" she said.

So I looked back up. She set the three bags on the table and then pointed to each one.

"A ball. A pump. And a spare," she said.

I blinked. "A spare what?" I asked.

"Ball!" she said. "In case I pop another one."

I frowned.

"Maybe you should be more careful with the first ball, so you don't need to buy the second and third balls," I said.

My mother made a huffing sound and grabbed the bags off the table.

"You sound just like your father. Inflatable balls weren't meant to last forever. You're supposed to replace them every now and then," she said.

While that might have been true, my mom had only had her first ball, the one that popped, for a few weeks. And now she had two more. That seemed like a lot.

"Is that another bag?" I asked. "A fourth one?"

I could see a small plastic bag tucked inside one of the other bags.

"It's just an empty box," she said.

But I knew that trick. That was a half-truth.

"But what was inside it before it was empty?" I asked.

My mother smiled. Then she reached in her purse.

"A new cell phone!" she said.

This was terrible. Because my father had once told me that new electronics cost an arm and a leg.

"Wait until you hear my ringtone," she said.

She hurried to the kitchen phone and dialed her cell phone number. But it didn't make a ringing sound. It chirped. And made a pounding noise. And chirped again.

"What is it?" I asked. "It sounds like a parakeet. And a hammer."

"It does not sound like a parakeet and a hammer!" my mother said. "It's the song of the red-bellied woodpecker. That's always been my favorite bird."

"Are you sure?" I asked. "I didn't know you had a favorite bird."

"Well, I do," she said, folding the phone shut and sliding it back inside her purse. "I love my new ringtone. And part of the purchase price for my phone is being donated to a red-bellied woodpecker sanctuary."

"Oh," I said. I was beginning to think that my mother couldn't leave the house without buying something. Like maybe she had an illness. I put my head down and focused on spelling.

"What are you working on?" she asked.

"Diphthongs," I said.

"What?" she asked.

I cleared my throat. "When two vowels join together to make one sound, it's called a diphthong. Like in *poison* or *trapezoid*," I said.

My mother tilted her head to one side and all of her curls slid in that direction.

"*Trapezoid* is on your spelling list?" she asked.

I nodded. My mother slapped the table.

"If your teacher wants to keep assigning advanced material, he should just go back to the sixth grade where he belongs."

I kept working. Even though my mother's slap made the table wobble.

"I like Mr. Hawk," I said.

"Well, he and I might need to have another discussion," she said.

I quit working and looked up. My eyes grew very huge and I shook my head.

"Camille, it tortures me to watch you struggle like this," she said.

"Really?" I asked.

"Absolutely. As a parent, I want to do anything I can to help you. It's a mother's animal instinct."

This surprised me very much. Because I had never thought of my mother as being a "mother animal." I'd only thought of her as being a fighting wolverine.

"Well, if that's true, why don't you call Dad," I said. "Because not having him here makes me struggle a lot."

She took a deep breath.

"Camille, that's not what I meant," she said. "I meant I could fix things with Mr. Hawk."

"But I don't think there's anything there that needs to be fixed," I said.

"That man is treating you like you're twelve," she said. "His actions could impact your development."

I set my pencil down.

"I don't worry about that," I said. "But I do worry about how well I'll develop without Dad around."

"Camille, your father and I are going through a rough patch. Things are going to have to work themselves out," she said.

"Maybe a phone call could help that," I said.

"No," my mother said.

But then, like magic, the phone started ringing.

"Aren't you going to get that?" I asked.

My mother walked to the kitchen phone and pulled it out of its cradle.

"I'm doing fine," she said. "Yes, I have seen the Visa bill for this month."

I gathered up my homework. I hated to hear them go through the Visa bill. I decided to go downstairs to watch some television and maybe do some looking at our house's guts. Upstairs, I heard yelling. And the sound of my mother's feet as she paced through the kitchen.

Downstairs, on CNN, they showed a big crowd of people in Japan. This made me a little bit excited, because they said that it was "live" television. And I thought I could look for Sally and possibly see her live. I stood very close to the TV. But nobody looked like

Sally. The whole crowd appeared to be people I didn't know. I thought about turning the channel. But I decided to look harder.

Then, in the corner, I spotted somebody who looked familiar. Could it be? Was it her? The person who looked familiar stood next to a tree. Which was exactly where I would expect to find Sally Zook. Because she loved trees. In the summer, she climbed them all the time.

"Turn around!" I said to the television. Because I wanted to know if the person really was Sally.

Whoever it was looked happy. Though I couldn't see her actual face. But I could see that she was carrying a purple purse. Then she started walking away. Right off the screen. Seeing this made me think of a lot of questions for Sally. *Why aren't you writing me? Don't you miss me? And when did you get a purple purse? And what do you keep inside it?* I stared at that crowd in Japan until the screen changed.

CNN switched to a picture of a turtle that had two heads. It was so ugly I turned off the TV, climbed the stairs, and went to my room. I felt so sad. I heard my mother still going over the Visa bill.

"The charge I made at Kmart was for a hot glue gun," she said. "We needed it."

I put my pillow over my head. And then I closed my eyes. And waited for dinner.

The next day, when I got to school, I arrived ready for Technology. It was not my favorite class, because it involved following directions *exactly*. And I enjoyed only following directions *somewhat*.

"Please sit at your assigned computer," Mr. Hawk said.

This meant that I had to sit next to Nina Hosack.

"Today we're going to be sending e-mails to other students," Mr. Hawk said. "Go ahead and open up your accounts."

So I used my mouse to click what I needed to, and got into my account. "Today you're going to be sending an e-mail to the person on your right," Mr. Hawk said. I looked at Nina and nodded. But when I looked to my left, which is the direction my e-mail would be coming from, all I saw was a wall. Because I was the last person in the row.

"Camille, you'll be getting an e-mail from Polly," Mr. Hawk said. "Go ahead and send the person on your right one question. Don't forget to spell-check before you send."

The whole class started clicking keys.

This was my question to Nina:

Do you have a dog?

This was my question from Polly:

What's inside your cooler?

When everybody stopped pecking at the keys, Mr. Hawk gave us more instructions. "Go ahead and answer the question. And then send one question back to the person who asked you a question."

I took many deep breaths. Then I wrote Polly back.

Lots of things are in my cooler. Cheese. Fruit. Ham. My blood is the kind that spikes. And crashes.

Question to Polly:

Have you ever been on a plane?

Answer from Nina:

I don't have a dog. I am allergic to all fur. And when I take baths, I have to use a special bar of soap.

Wow. I wanted to write back to Nina that she'd given me too much information. But I didn't. I just looked at her and said, "Too bad about the special soap."

Polly's answer made me laugh.

I have been on a plane. I have been to
Florida. And Texas. And New York. And
Italy. I liked it. Because you get to
fly above the clouds. Did you know that
on planes they have a barf bag for
every seat? It's true!

I peeked my head over my computer and looked at
Polly.

"I didn't know they had a barf bag for every seat,"
I said. "Is there that much barfing on planes?"

"There wasn't on mine," Polly said. "But I took my
barf bag with me as a souvenir. They're free."

"Cool!" I said.

"You could come and see it," she said. "I still have it."

And so I nodded. But I wasn't sure I wanted to do
that. Because spending time together meant we would
be friends. But sending e-mails in Technology didn't
mean anything, because it was an assignment.

"What kind of cheese do you eat?" Polly asked me.

"String," I said. "Hey, you type really fast."

"I send a lot of e-mails," she said.

And this made me feel a little bad. Because I didn't
send very many e-mails. At home, I didn't have an account. I only had one at school. But I guess that was okay.
Because typing was hard. But talking on the phone was
easy. And who would I send an e-mail to anyway?

CHAPTER 19

OPPORTUNITY KNOCKS

I think Mr. Hawk forgot that he told us to count all our lightbulbs. Because a few days after he told us to do that, he never asked how many lightbulbs we had. But that was okay. Because I kept forgetting to count them anyway. So if he asked, I was going to have to make up a number and say that my house had one thousand three hundred seventy-six lightbulbs. Because I didn't want to look poor.

"Time for science," Mr. Hawk said.

He stood up and licked his thumb. Then he peeled papers off a thick pile and sent them down our rows.

"I'm very excited to share something today," Mr. Hawk said.

"Is this about our lightbulbs?" Penny asked.

"No. This is about an opportunity. For the first time ever, the Rocky Mountain Middle School Science Fair has offered a special category for young scientists."

I had no idea what this had to do with us. Because we weren't middle school students. Also, we weren't young scientists.

"Normally, I end the month of April by having each student pair up with another student and give a presentation about groundwater and pollution and the hydrologic cycle."

I was very surprised to hear Mr. Hawk say this. Because that sounded like the most advanced project ever. And I thought he and my mom had come to an understanding.

"But this year, for a change of pace, I think it would be a good idea to let you take part in the Rocky Mountain Middle School Science Fair. The grand-prize winner of the fair receives fifty dollars and is eligible to enter the District Ninety-three Science Fair. And the District 93 Science Fair winner is eligible for the Idaho

State Science Fair. And the Idaho State Science Fair winner is eligible for the national science fair, which has a five-thousand-dollar grand prize."

As Mr. Hawk spoke, he raised his winglike arms to his sides. My mother had told me that raising your arms like that was an excellent way to work out your medial deltoids.

"But we're not in middle school," Lilly said.

"This year, there is a new category. Young scientists from fourth to sixth grades can enter. I've made copies of the rules. Your projects will be due in two weeks," Mr. Hawk said.

When he said five thousand dollars, my mind started zooming a million miles an hour. Because if I won five thousand dollars, I could buy thousands of minutes to talk to Sally. And maybe I could even help my parents pay their Visa bill. And maybe I'd have enough money left over to visit Sally in Japan and fly on a plane and get my own free barf bag.

"As a class, we're only allowed to enter a limited number of projects, so I want you to work in pairs. Please write down your name and the name of the person you'd like to work with and hand it in. I'll assign groups tomorrow."

We all started scribbling. I got very nervous. I didn't know who to put down. Finally, I wrote *Penny Winchester*. Because she came from a farm, so she probably knew a lot about science. Because I always thought of science as involving dirt.

I grabbed all my homework and walked out to the bus. I thought I was going to have to avoid Polly. But I didn't. Because she and Hannah Pond were walking together.

I stayed behind them. And that didn't bother me. Because Aunt Stella had told me the rule about moving. And if Polly took planes to visit Texas and Florida and New York and Italy, she seemed like a flight risk anyway. A picture of Emily Santa giving her report on brown tree snakes flashed through my mind. It sent a shiver through me. I didn't understand how moving could be so easy for grown-ups. But it was. Here today, Guam tomorrow.

When I got off the bus, I spotted my mom kneeling down next to our house, pulling weeds out of our flower bed.

"How was school?" she asked.

Instead of telling her about the science fair, I decided not to mention it. Because if she knew we were being asked to build a project for a young-scientist program, she might go talk to Mr. Hawk and the whole thing could get called off and then I wouldn't win any money.

"Fine," I said.

"Now that your father isn't around, it's up to us to

do the yard work. Do you want to help me?" my mom asked.

I shook my head.

"I need some cottage cheese," I said.

When I went inside, I didn't want cottage cheese anymore. I wanted to talk to Aunt Stella. So I called her really quickly. But I dialed wrong and got a pet store instead.

"Sorry!" I said.

And then I calmed down and dialed more slowly.

"I've been thinking about you a lot," Aunt Stella said. "How are you?"

"I'm okay. Aunt Stella, did you know that on airplanes they have a barf bag for every seat? And that if you want to take your barf bag with you, even if you haven't barfed in it, it's free?"

"I did know that," Aunt Stella said.

"It makes me want to ride on an airplane," I said.

"I bet one day you do," she said. "How are other things going?"

"Well, Mom is doing yard work because Dad is still out of town. Also, we had a very big Visa bill this month," I said.

"Your parents show you the Visa bill?" she asked.

"No. They just yell about it," I said.

"Camille, you should not be worried about things like that. You should be focused on school. And friends."

"Yeah," I said.

"You sound like you have something on your mind," Aunt Stella said.

"Well, I have been thinking about something," I said.

"What?" she asked.

"How old were you when you got a purse?"

"Oh, I don't remember," she said.

"Were you my age?" I asked.

"No. I didn't start carrying a purse until I was in high school," she said.

"Oh," I said.

"You sound so sad. Was that the wrong answer?" she asked.

"No," I said.

But really I was feeling pretty terrible that Sally had only been gone eight and a half months, but she was carrying a purse around and acting like a totally different person. Then I heard a beeping sound because I was getting another call.

"I need to answer that," I said. "It could be my dad. And I haven't talked to him since he drove off and left us."

"Okay. I love you, Camille," Aunt Stella said.

"Me too," I said.

Then I answered the other call.

"Hello?" I asked.

"Camille!" my father cheered, "How are you?"

"I'm okay," I said.

"I miss you so much," he said.

"Me too," I said.

"What? You miss yourself?" he asked.

"No, I miss you," I said.

"I know. I was joking," he said. "So what have you been up to?"

"I've been learning about technology and barf bags, and also I've been assigned the role of a cat in the school play."

"A cat!" my father said. "How exciting. You love cats."

"Yeah. But I have to stand on a plastic bucket and drown," I said.

"Are you sure?" my father asked. "That doesn't sound good."

"Yeah. It's because the world has too many cats. And our play is about teaching people to be more responsible with their cats and their factories."

"Your play is about cat factories?"

"No," I sighed, rolling my eyes. "Our play is about a world that isn't sunny anymore. Because all the factories make it rainy. And so to save all the animals, Nora drives her bus and takes them from the zoo. Except cats don't live in the zoo. Because they are wild and homeless and so they live wherever they want. And there's too many of them to fit on the bus. So they die."

"I don't think I've ever heard of that play," he said.

"Mrs. Zirklezack wrote it," I said.

"Sounds heavy," he said.

I shrugged.

"Are you still there, Camille?" he asked.

"Yes," I said.

"Well, I've got to wrap this up. I'm on my way to Portland and I want to beat traffic. I was just calling to tell you that I love you."

"Don't you want to talk to Mom? She's outside doing yard work, but I could get her," I said.

"That's okay," he said. "I was calling to talk to you."

"Oh," I said.

"I'll call again soon. I love you!" he said.

"I love you too," I said. And then I hung up the stupid phone. And tried not to cry. And decided to go to my room and read all about the Rocky Mountain Middle School Science Fair. Because hearing about it had been the brightest spot in my day.

CHAPTER 20

big PlANS

The next day I was very excited to find out who my science partner was. But I became a lot less excited when I bumped into Mrs. Zirklezack at the drinking fountain.

"I'm on my way to your classroom," she said.

And then we walked there together.

"These are for the cats," she said, handing some papers to Mr. Hawk. She pulled one piece off the pile and handed it to me.

"It outlines the parameters for your cat costumes," she said.

"Oh," I said. Because I wasn't sure what *parameters* meant.

Mr. Hawk read the paper too.

"Looks like you can make your costume out of anything you want. As long as you have black ears, a black unitard, and a black tail," he said.

I nodded.

"And a clean face," Mrs. Zirklezack said. "I'll be painting them the day of the show."

"My face is usually pretty clean," I said.

"Fantastic!" Mrs. Zirklezack said, and then she left.

Once we were all seated, Mr. Hawk stood up and rubbed his chin.

"I bet you're all very excited to hear about your science fair partners," he said. "So I'm going to start with that. Let me begin by saying that I wasn't able to honor every partner request."

I did not enjoy hearing that. Then he started listing all the names of people in my class.

"Polly is with Hannah. Tony is with Boone. Penny is with Lilly. Zoey is with Gracie. Nina is with Camille—"

And then I stopped listening. Because I'd just been assigned Nina Hosack, a chubby, pigtailed, overly clean blonde.

Nina looked at me and waved. But I didn't wave back. I covered my mouth in horror. I'd just been paired with the galaxy's biggest wimp. Looking at her pale, gluelike, milky face from across the room, I didn't think she was capable of winning a science fair.

"Go ahead and take the next few minutes to brainstorm with your partner about possible projects," Mr. Hawk said.

"I'll come to you, Camille. So you don't have to move your cooler," Nina said.

I closed my eyes. And when I opened them again, Nina was standing right there.

"First, we're assigned to be cats together. Then, we send each other e-mails in Technology. And now we're paired up as science partners. Isn't that cool?" Nina asked me.

I decided to ignore that question.

"Do you have any ideas?" I asked.

"No," she said.

I let out a big breath.

"Not even bad ideas?" I asked.

"Maybe we could show the class a worm," Nina said.

"Really?" I asked. "You're willing to touch a worm?"

"Worms are good for the earth. They help it breathe," Nina said. "Even though they're disgusting, I can appreciate them."

"Wow," I said. "Good to know. But how is bringing a worm to school a science project?"

"Maybe we could point out all the worm's parts," Nina said.

"Ooh," I said. "And then maybe we could cut it in two in front of the class, because I heard you can do that to a worm."

Nina screamed. I guess that idea was too much for her.

"Is everything okay over there?" Mr. Hawk asked.

"We're deciding on a project," I said.

"Do you need any help?" he asked.

"Lots," Nina said.

"Some," I said.

"Well, when it comes to deciding on a project, I think it's important to think about what you love. Ask yourself this question: 'What interests me?' "

"I think Nina and I have different interests," I said.

Mr. Hawk put his hands in his pockets and kept talking.

"Okay. Try to have a discussion. Do either of you have any problems that you want science to solve? What do you love? What do you spend your energy dreaming about? That should really be your focus," he said. "Follow your heart." And then he patted his heart three times.

"Thanks," Nina said. "That helped."

Mr. Hawk walked away.

"I guess that means no worm," Nina said. "Because I don't dream about them and they do nothing for my heart."

"Okay," I said. "What do you love?"

"Marshmallows, potato chips, and dollhouse furniture," Nina said.

I felt sick to my stomach. Out of all the things Nina loved, only the marshmallows seemed to have any science-project potential.

"Maybe we should sleep on this," I said. "And then talk on the phone."

"We can talk in class," Nina said.

"The phone is better for me," I said. And I didn't know why that was the truth. But it was.

Mr. Hawk told us to wrap it up because we had to move on to spelling. I watched Nina walk back to her desk and sit down.

Marshmallows? Potato chips? Dollhouse furniture? I took out my spelling worksheets and tried not to feel totally rotten.

When I got home, I felt awful and needed a banana. But there was bad news: We were out of them. But there was also good news: My mom was punching the air in the kitchen. And she had a list of groceries she needed taped to the refrigerator. So maybe we could go to the store.

"Peekaboo! Jab! Jab!" she cried.

I waved my arms in front of her.

"Bananas!" I said.

She stopped punching. Sweat beads splattered onto the linoleum floor.

"Bananas?" she asked.

"We're out."

"Camille, you eat a lot of bananas," she said. "It makes me believe in evolution."

"What?" I asked.

"It's a theory that says we descended from apes."

I rolled my eyes. "That explains a lot," I said. But really, I didn't think that it explained anything. I pointed to the note on the refrigerator.

"We're out of a lot of things," I said.

"Only tuna fish, pickles, and paper towels," she said.

"We should go to the store," I said.

"Do you need something besides bananas?" my mother asked.

And when she said that, I realized that I did need something besides bananas. I needed an international calling card!

My mother loved to go to the store. And I knew she'd probably take me too. But I didn't tell her about my plans to buy a calling card. I figured that was my business.

"Let's go to a superstore," I said. Because those places sell everything. Even tires and diamond rings.

"Sounds good," my mom said.

Once we were at the superstore, my mother said she needed to assess the Lycra content of some socks. That did not seem fun or necessary. I took off and told her I would meet her by the bananas. She didn't object.

I hurried to the electronics section where they had a whole rack of calling cards. They had all sorts of countries that I was unfamiliar with, like Algeria and Swaziland. And they were not in any order. I hunted to find Japan. It was next to Yemen, which I thought was weird.

Sadly, I couldn't afford a hundred minutes. Due to some recent spending, and because I liked to keep five emergency dollars in my underwear drawer, I only had about sixty dollars to spend. And to talk to Sally in Japan cost two dollars a minute. I thought that was a rip-off. But I needed the card. So I bought it. It came with a lot of instructions that I did not have time to read. I handed it to the man working at the register.

"What's this?" the man asked me. He wore a bright blue smock and a pin that said FRED.

"My international calling card," I said. I lifted up my money to show Fred that I had it.

"An international calling card?" he asked. He took my money and frowned. "You're not trying to contact some stranger you met on the Internet, are you? That would be dangerous."

He gave me back a few pennies in change and my calling card.

"I've never met any strangers on the Internet," I said. "I only e-mail people in my row."

"Then why do you need an international calling card?" he asked.

I wanted to tell Fred that it was none of his business. But I was afraid he might make me get my mother.

"I'm going to call my very good friend Sally who lives in Japan. She moved there in September," I said. "I miss her."

"I see," Fred said. "I hope you two have a good talk."

I smiled.

"Me too," I said. I hadn't realized that the electronics counter was such a friendly place.

I stuck my calling card in my pocket along with the receipt and went to look for my mother near the bananas.

Walking through the superstore, I had a terrible thought. What if Polly was in the superstore? What if I ran into her? I looked around. I didn't see her. That was a good thing. Because if I did, she probably would have asked me what I was doing. But I wouldn't have told her. Because it was none of her business. And she probably would've told me that she was at the superstore buying catnip for her cat or something.

Because that's just like Polly. Always talking about how she had a cat and a barf bag and I didn't. I found my mother holding three huge bunches of bananas.

"Will these be enough?" she asked.

"I'm not a gorilla."

"I think gorillas are meat eaters," she said, setting the bananas in the cart. "I don't think they eat bananas. I think they'll even eat each other."

That didn't sound right.

"No," I said. "Gorillas are herbivores. And they're shy. And smart. You can teach a gorilla sign language. They even have fingerprints. I saw a show about them."

My mother blinked at me like she was surprised to learn this.

"Once, at the circus, I saw a chimpanzee operate a motorbike," she said. "Vroom, vroom."

But I didn't know what that had to do with what I'd said about gorillas. The thought of my mother seeing that sort of thing at a circus made me sad. Because it was wrong to put a chimpanzee on a motorbike and make it go vroom vroom. Just like it was wrong to put cats on plastic buckets and make them dance and sing during a rainstorm. Riding home in the car, thinking about this, I thought of two other things that were wrong with the world. My favorite aunt didn't belong all the way in Modesto. And my parents did not belong apart.

CHAPTER 21

MAKEUP AND INSPIRATION

Nina and I talked on the phone every night for a whole week. But we couldn't think of a project.

"We're running out of time," Nina said.

"I'm aware of that," I said.

"Our project is due in ten days," she said.

"I'm aware of that, too," I said.

"Maybe we could do something with ice," Nina said.

"Like what?" I asked.

"I don't know," Nina said.

"What about goats?" I asked. "I really like goats."

"But I'm allergic to all fur," she said.

"Right," I said. "Plus, you use special soap."

"Have you asked your mother for ideas?" Nina asked.

"No," I said. Then I thought it might be a good idea to tell Nina the truth about something. "Nina, we should never mention this project to my mother."

"Why?" Nina asked.

"My mother is not a fan of advanced science," I said.

"Really?" she asked.

"Yes. And if she finds out about the science fair, you'll be doing this project alone," I said.

"Wow," Nina said. "I won't say anything."

"Good," I said. "Do you have any other ideas?"

"Maybe we could do something with magnets," Nina said.

"Like what?" I asked.

"I don't know. Maybe we could attach them to marshmallows," Nina said. "And heat them up."

I sighed. "That's not science, Nina," I said. "That's making s'mores that you can't eat because they have magnets in them."

"You're right," Nina said. "I can't think of anything else."

"Okay," I said. "I'll call you again tomorrow."

When I got off the phone I stomped into the living room. I didn't know we had company.

"Camille," my mother said. "This is Beatrice. She's our Avon Lady."

"Hi," I said.

The woman was wearing very red lipstick. And she was in the process of putting that same very red lipstick on my mother.

"Do you like makeup, Camille?" Beatrice asked. "I'm giving your mother a makeover."

My mother laughed. I thought her lips made her look like she had a clown mouth.

"Camille is too young for makeup," my mother said.

I watched Beatrice brush pink powder on my mother's cheeks.

"This rose tone brings out your eyes," Beatrice said.

"I just want something easy," my mother said. "Something I don't have to slave over in the morning."

"How about no makeup?" I said. "That's the easiest. And the cheapest."

My mother frowned at me.

"Makeup is essential," Beatrice said. As she spoke, she pointed the brush at me. I saw a huge ring on her finger that looked like a tooth.

"What is that?" I asked.

"A blush brush," Beatrice said.

"No, on your hand," I said.

Beatrice looked at her ring and smiled.

"It's an elk tooth," she said. And then she kept putting blush on my mother.

"Camille, close your mouth," my mother said.

I did. Then I asked a question.

"Why are you wearing an elk tooth?" I asked.

"It's a gift from my husband," she said. "He wears one too. We're bowhunters."

And I knew that if you were a bowhunter it meant that you went into the wilderness, usually Montana, and shot animals like deer and elk with a bow and arrow.

"You kill elk and make jewelry out of their teeth?" I asked. Because I was beginning to think that our Avon Lady was a weirdo.

"It was the first elk we took down together," she said. "It was special. So we decided to save some sort of relic."

"Oh," I said.

"Do you know what a relic is?" Beatrice asked.

I shook my head.

"Well, a relic is a very special object. It's sacred," she said.

And I thought it was pretty awful that she'd killed a sacred elk. But then Beatrice explained a lot more about relics. She said that they were objects that had been saved, mostly for religious reasons, for hundreds and hundreds of years.

"Do they bring luck?" I asked.

"I think they do," she said.

Beatrice winked at me and then turned back to my mother. And kept slathering makeup on her.

"I have to wear makeup for our school play," I said. "I'm a cat."

"Well, one day you'll want to wear makeup to accentuate your features and hide your flaws."

"You mean my freckles?" I asked. "Because I only have nine."

My mother laughed. And that made it harder for Beatrice to stick makeup on her.

"Camille, you might not realize this now, but your face matters. A woman's appearance is her calling card."

And I didn't say anything else. Because the words *calling card* made my mind zoom to Sally. And this made me tingle with happiness. I stood and watched Beatrice tap her brush on her hand and then outline my mother's eyes.

"Maybe you should take a nap," my mother said.

"A nap?" I asked.

My mother hadn't suggested that I take a nap in almost three years.

"You look tired," she said.

And after she said that, I did feel a little sleepy. Worrying about my science project all week was hard work. And so was play practice. We were now to the point that we had to stand on our buckets during our song. We weren't allowed to just stand next to them, because Mrs. Zirklezack said that we needed to strengthen our balancing muscles.

Resting on my bed, looking at my ceiling, I tried to think of a good project. I wondered what Polly was making. I wondered what Penny was going to build. I thought and thought. And then I fell asleep. That's when I had a nap dream. Muffin came and found me and sat on my chest. At first, I thought it was Checkers. But then Muffin reminded me that he had orange on his face and body and that Checkers didn't. I was so happy to have Muffin back. Plus, it was nice that Muffin could finally talk to me.

"I miss you, Camille," he said. "We used to have so much fun together."

"I know," I said. "I wish you were still around. You were very special."

"Yes," he said. "I know."

When I woke up, even though it was almost night, I ran to the phone and called Nina.

"What is it?" Nina asked.

"I can't tell you right now," I said. Then I whispered, "I can't talk about advanced science at the moment."

"Is your mom right there?" Nina asked.

"Yes," I said.

"Do you have an idea for our project?" Nina asked.

"I do," I said.

"Why don't you come over to my house on Friday and we can get started?" Nina said.

"We have to do it at my house," I said.

"But what if your mom sees us?" Nina asked.

"We'll be in my backyard," I said. "She won't see anything."

"Does our project involve marshmallows?" Nina asked.

"No," I said.

"Magnets?" Nina asked.

"No," I said.

"What does it involve?" Nina asked.

"Shovels," I said.

CHAPTER 22

the Dig

All week long, Nina kept asking me nosy questions about our science project.

"Are you sure it doesn't have worms in it?" she asked.

"Yes," I said.

"Why did you say it involved shovels?" she asked.

"Because it does," I said.

"But worms live in the dirt!" she said.

"Look," I said. "Our project doesn't involve worms. But it does involve dirt. So we might possibly see one worm."

"I just want to be prepared," Nina said.

I didn't tell Nina about the project because I was afraid she'd object. I didn't lay it on her until Friday on the bus.

Three stops before my house, I filled her in on the plan. She seemed confused and a little bit freaked out. But when I asked her if she knew how many potato chips, marshmallows, and pieces of doll furniture half of five thousand dollars would buy, her eyes grew wide and twinkled a little bit, and she finally agreed.

When Nina and I got off the bus, we went inside to meet my mother. The Avon Lady had left a lasting mark. My mother now wore green eye shadow. It wasn't very dark. But it was still green.

"It's nice to meet you, Nina," my mother said. "Do you want anything to eat?"

Nina shook her head. I think our science project made her lose her appetite.

"We're going to play outside," I said.

My mother smiled. "Have fun."

After we left my mother to work out in the den, I led Nina straight to the garage and handed her a shovel. I told her to follow me. Nina did not have very strong muscles in her arms. When she tried to walk with her shovel, the handle kept bumping her in the forehead. After a few bumps, she finally spoke.

"This feels like a bad idea," she said, purposely walking slower than I wanted.

I tuned her out and kept walking. Because my idea was the best idea either one of us had had.

We made our way across my backyard, through my mother's freshly rototilled garden, and into the field, overgrown with weeds. I led her to the pile of stones that propped up Muffin's Popsicle-stick cross. Because it had sentimental value, I carefully slid the cross into my back pocket.

"This is the place," I said, striking the blade of my shovel into the ground. Because Muffin was so special, I thought a great project would be to bring his bones to class. And talk about them. And I thought I knew exactly how to do this. Because on the Science Channel, I'd seen paleontologists unearth a bunch of graves, and brush the dirt off the bones, and find the skeletons looking almost perfect.

"How long has your cat been dead?" Nina asked, struggling to push the head of her own shovel into the earth.

"Two years," I said. "He never saw the mail truck coming." I lifted a big scoop of dirt out of the hole. Two years was plenty of time, I thought, for even a good-sized cat to be reduced to bones.

Muffin had been an excellent tabby. Unlike Fluff, my cat before him, Muffin never used his claws. And he enjoyed being indoors, sunbathing on windowsills, and watching birds on television. And unlike Checkers, my cat before Fluff, Muffin never strayed far from home. I wasn't sure why I was so unlucky with cats. Even when I whistled at stray cats, they always ran away from me. (Cats are very good runners.)

Nina kicked at the mound of growing dirt with the toe of her sneaker.

"We could build a volcano out of clay and attach it to batteries," she said.

This idea had been written at the bottom of the science fair instructions. Everybody had read it. That meant it wasn't a good idea anymore.

"That won't win. That's what people build who don't have good ideas," I said.

"Okay," she said.

Nina may have been a wimp, but she was a pretty good digger. Even better than me.

"Hey, I've struck plastic," Nina said, taking her shovel out of the hole.

This was very exciting. I put on my mother's weeding gloves and reached down. I scooped at the loose dirt, uncovering the bag.

"Help me," I said, pulling the garbage bag out of the ground.

Nina put on her gloves too and reached down with me. Together we lifted the heavy sack out of the grave.

"Why does this weigh so much?" Nina asked, dropping her end.

That was a good question. I didn't know why Muffin's bones were so heavy. I tried to make something up.

"Mud must have gotten inside," I said, carefully resting my side on the long grass. Moist dirt clung to folds in the dark green plastic near the twist-tied top. The sack was bigger than I'd remembered.

Nina looked green and scared. Even though it was obvious what was going to happen next, she acted like she had no idea what to expect.

"We need to open it up," I said.

"This isn't safe. I want to wear goggles."

Nina folded her arms across her chest and shook her blond, pigtailed head back and forth.

I frowned. Nina was such a drag. Finding goggles would take time. If my mother found out we'd borrowed her gloves or gardening tools to dig up Muffin, she'd be unhappy, even concerned. Not only was she on the lookout for signs of "advanced science," but ever since my dad left, my mother had been also watching me more closely. On the phone with her friends, she had even begun referring to me as a preteen.

I poked at the bag with my gloved fingers. In between spots of soft mush, I could feel Muffin's hard bones. His skeleton felt jumbled up, like most of the bones were out of order.

"It's safe," I assured her.

"How are you going to break the plastic?" Nina asked.

I showed her my pocketknife. She shook her head again. I knelt down on the grass and decided where I should make my cut.

"I think I smell something," Nina said.

I thought I smelled something too. Something nasty. But like a true paleontologist, I pressed on. I held the knife in my right hand and pinched my nose with my left. As I put my knife to the plastic, I heard a soft bark and then a crunching noise. When I looked up, I saw Pinky, Mr. Lively's spotless, pink-nosed, deaf, albino Dalmatian, darting through my mother's garden toward us. Nina dropped her shovel and screamed.

"Don't run," I warned. "He'll chase you. He'll bite." Rarely was Pinky aggressive, but when he was a puppy he had nipped my mother's gloved hand. And last week, as the Avon Lady was leaving, Pinky had sunk his teeth into her briefcase and tugged.

"That beast should be muzzled," the Avon Lady had snapped, inspecting the tear marks on her leather case where Pinky had hooked his teeth.

I was sure that the reason Pinky had bit my

mother's gloved hand and the Avon Lady's case was because he knew that they were made out of leather and somehow Pinky's nose knew that leather came from cows. On some level, I thought, Pinky thought he was biting a cow.

"Don't run!" I yelled again. I wasn't sure how much leather Nina was wearing, but I did know that Pinky was a dog, and a dog was an animal, and all animals liked to chase things, especially things that were running away.

But Nina didn't listen. She sprang away from me and Pinky gave chase. I called for them to stop, but neither one did. Nina's blond pigtails and chubby belly bounced as she ran. It didn't take long for Pinky to catch up to her, knocking her to the ground. He wagged his tail happily, trying to lick her face.

Nina blocked his tongue with her arms. She curled her legs in to her stomach, trying to make herself into a ball, to protect every part of her against Pinky's paws and teeth.

"Does it have rabies?" she cried. "Is it foaming at the mouth?"

I tried to be perfectly honest.

"He probably doesn't have rabies," I said. "But he is foaming a little bit at the mouth."

"Ahhh!" Nina screamed.

Losing interest in Nina, the human ball, Pinky leapt

in my direction. He tore through the long grass, flattening the weeds as he ran. When he stopped in front of me, I reached out to pet him. But he tightened his body and growled. He lowered his wet nose to the sack and gave it several quick sniffs. Slobber dangled from his mouth.

"It'll eat Muffin!" Nina yelled. "Big dogs eat cats!" She stood up and ran back toward us.

Pinky pawed at the plastic, tearing it open in three ragged lines. Nina rushed to do something, but she tripped. She picked up her shovel but it tumbled from her hands and I watched the handle come down hard, swatting Pinky on the snout. He let out a cry, pain mixed with surprise, and then bolted through the field back home.

Nina caught her balance and picked her shovel back up. Using its blade, she nudged the bag back into the hole.

"This is the worst smell I've ever smelled in my whole life, Camille," she said. "I'm going home. I'm building a volcano."

The hem of her khaki pants and her shoes were caked with dirt. Her elbows, stained with grass, were red from her fall.

"I didn't plan it this way," I said, helping to move some dirt back over Muffin.

"Really, Camille. What were you thinking?"

Nina didn't look at me when she talked. She filled the hole and patted down the dirt with the back of her shovel.

"I don't know," I said.

Nina threw her shovel on the ground and turned toward my house. "It smells so rotten." She walked through the unplanted rows of corn, and passed a pile of seed potatoes my mother was getting ready to plant.

I didn't know what to do.

"Put my name on it too!" I called after her. "I'll buy the batteries."

CHAPTER 23

GUMDROPS

Nina Hosack may have been a chubby wimp, but she was an excellent walker. That day, she trudged three long miles to get home. She called to let me know she'd made it there safely.

"Is everything okay?" I asked.

I was hoping she'd give me useful information about the state of our volcano.

"I'll see you tomorrow," she said. And then she hung up on me. And after that happens, after somebody hangs up on you, there's really nothing more that you can say. Because there's just a dial tone.

That night, I flipped and flopped on my new mattress. All of my dreams were horrible. In them, nobody at school would talk to me because they said I smelled like a dead cat. Nina had told everybody. And I didn't do a very good job defending myself, because for some reason I showed up to school that day wearing only my underwear. I was too embarrassed to explain anything. All I could do was fold my arms across my chest and run away. That's how a lot of my dreams when I'm only wearing underwear end.

But the next day when I got to school, it turned out that Nina was a lot more mature than I realized. As soon as I saw her I gave her five dollars for the batteries. She took the bill, folded it up, slipped it in her pocket, and told me, "We're square, Camille."

I decided not to ask her about the volcano. I pretended like I didn't care. It was a nice break to pretend that my big problems didn't matter.

Then I turned a corner and saw something very marvelous. It was Ms. Golden. I was so happy to see her that I jumped up and down and ran in her direction.

"Ms. Golden! You're back!" I yelled.

And she let me hug her. I couldn't wait for math and social studies and health to end, so that I could head straight to gifted reading and my beanbag.

When Mr. Hawk dismissed us for gifted reading, I had a hard time not pushing ahead of everybody else and yelling, "Run! Run!"

"I wonder if Ms. Golden's voice changed," Penny said. "My uncle had his tonsils taken out and now he sounds like an otter."

This made me very curious.

"What does an otter sound like?" I asked.

Penny made a *bah* sound and pinched her throat and jiggled the skin on her neck.

"Ms. Golden doesn't sound like an otter," I said. "I talked to her this morning."

I thought when Ms. Golden got back that we'd read a folktale. But we didn't. We read "The Mouse at the Seashore," a fable written by Arnold Lobel. Before we started, Ms. Golden asked us to close our eyes and picture something that we really wanted. I didn't close my eyes right away. I looked at everybody else. Then Ms. Golden smiled at me, so I closed my eyes too.

As I pictured things that I really wanted, I was surprised at what popped into my head. Money. A hot dog. Sally. Jelly beans. But then I stopped thinking in pictures, and a whole movie played in my head. I was at the airport with my mom and dad. And we had tickets to fly somewhere. And I was eating cotton candy. . . .

But then Ms. Golden told us to open our eyes. And

my movie stopped playing before I found out where I was going.

"This is a story about a mouse," she said.

And I didn't think I was going to like it. Because I saw an actual mouse once, and it scared me so much that I jumped up onto a chair. But hearing about this mouse was kind of enjoyable. He wanted to visit the seashore. But the mouse's parents didn't want him to go. Because it was dangerous. But the mouse went anyway. He was almost eaten by a cat. And he got attacked by birds and dogs. But the mouse finally made it to the seashore. And he sat under the stars and watched the ocean. Then, Ms. Golden read the moral of the fable, which is the fable's message, something all fables have. "All the miles of a hard road are worth a moment of true happiness."

After Ms. Golden closed the book, she looked at us and asked us what we thought. But none of us said anything.

"Maybe this isn't the kind of story we talk about. Maybe this is the kind of story that we think about," Ms. Golden said.

We still didn't say anything.

"You've all gotten very quiet while I was away. Doesn't anybody have anything to say?"

"I didn't know a dog would go after a mouse like that," Jory said.

"I did!" Penny said. "My dog, Hustle, found an entire mouse nest in a field and ate them all!"

"That's terrible," Nina said.

"No it's not. Mice are vermin," Penny replied. "They eat our grain."

"Okay," Ms. Golden said. "Who wants to hear a fable about a bad kangaroo?"

And of course, we all raised our hands. Penny raised both of hers.

During lunch, I was expecting to sit at my fourth-grade table and eat my turkey sandwich and be mostly bored. But that's not what happened. Because Gracie Clop finally brought the picture of her grandpa feeding a grizzly bear a gumdrop.

"This is amazing!" Lilly said, before she passed it to Hannah.

"His hand is right by its mouth!" Hannah cried.

"I want to see it," Tony said.

"Be careful not to get your taco on it," Gracie said.

Tony wiped his hands on his pants and took the photo by its corner.

"This isn't a grizzly bear!" Tony said. "It doesn't have a hump."

Gracie snatched the photo out of Tony's hand.

"It does too," Gracie said.

Then she passed the photo to Polly. I leaned over and looked at it too.

"It's a black bear," Tony said. "Anybody could feed a gumdrop to a black bear."

"That's not true," Gracie said.

Polly passed the picture to Zoey.

"Everybody knows that grizzly bears claw your guts out. But black bears lick your face," Tony said.

"You're making that up!" Gracie said.

"No I'm not. My dad hunts. I've gone with him. I know *a lot* about bears," Tony said. "I thought your picture was going to be really amazing. But it was just okay."

"My picture *is* really amazing! Plus, my grandpa is really amazing. And that grizzly bear is really amazing," Gracie said. "The only person who isn't really amazing is you."

She sounded so upset that I thought she might throw some of her lunch at Tony. Boone took the picture and looked at it.

"Tell her it isn't a grizzly bear," Tony said to Boone.

Boone squinted. "I don't know what kind of bear it is. But I think the picture is really amazing."

Tony shook his head and stood up. Boone stayed seated. He passed the picture back to Gracie.

"I brought something for everybody," Gracie said. She reached into her lunch bag and pulled out a Baggie filled with gumdrops.

"Yay!" Nina said. "Gumdrops are my favorite."

I wanted to remind Nina that marshmallows and

potato chips were her favorites. But I didn't. When the bag reached me, I pulled out an orange gumdrop.

"Is it safe for you to eat sugar?" Polly asked me.

I frowned at her. Who did she think she was? My mother?

"It's okay if I eat just one," I said. And then, even though I wanted a green one, too, I passed the bag to Lilly.

CHAPTER 24

DOOM

Why couldn't I be a platypus? Or a snowy egret? Or an armadillo? I could think of a bunch of animals that weren't even assigned. Penny noticed this too. After practice, she bravely pointed out to Mrs. Zirklezack that several important zoo animals had been left out. But Mrs. Zirklezack had a quick answer.

"I didn't create a perfect heroine," Mrs. Zirklezack said. "Nora can't save everyone."

Penny sighed and walked away. That was the end of it.

All day long, even after I ate a piece of cheese, my mood sank lower and lower. *A drowned cat,* I said to myself over and over. When saying the word *drowned* no longer upset me, I borrowed Mr. Hawk's thesaurus. A *ruined* cat. A *doomed* cat. A *marked* cat. An *ill-fated* cat. A feline with *bad kismet.* I let these words bounce around in my brain. This worked. I became very sad again.

I was worried that there was something about me that looked doomed. Maybe it was my cooler. I wasn't sure. But there was one thing I grew more and more sure of during each play practice. If I really were living in a rainy world, I was pretty sure that I'd be one of the first animals on Nora's bus. Unless my white plastic bucket could also be used as a flotation device, I just couldn't picture myself standing on top of it dancing and singing. It just wasn't me. At heart, I knew I was a survivor. Wasn't I?

My legs felt as heavy as sandbags as I stepped off the bus. Crossing the road, I realized that I was crossing it alone. No Polly. No Danny. No Manny. Sadness gets worse when you're by yourself. I walked down my long driveway, kicking at the gravel. Then it hit me. I didn't have to be alone. I could call Sally. Because I had an international calling card!

First, I went to find my mother. She wasn't in the den. Or the kitchen. But she hadn't left a note either. She had never gone anywhere without leaving a note.

I felt nervous. And then I heard a rumbling noise. It sounded like our lawn mower. I looked out the kitchen window. My mother was attempting to cut the grass. That's something that my dad usually did. But since he was gone, our grass had gotten longer than our ankles. She was only halfway done and she did not look like she was enjoying herself. A cloud of dark smoke hung over her and the mower. I hoped it made her miss my dad more.

I went into my sock drawer and found the card and the instructions. I think the person who wrote the instructions must have thought people who used calling cards were stupid, because the instructions began by explaining all the numbers on the phone's keypad. I skipped the instructions and decided to try to call information in Japan.

To use my calling card, I had to enter a lot of numbers. And after I did that, a woman with a robot voice would repeat what I'd entered and ask me to press 8 for yes and 9 for no. Because I didn't make any mistakes, I ended up pressing 8 a lot. I also had to look inside the phone book to try to figure out how to dial Information in Japan.

I found the ski trails for Sun Valley. I found the seating map for Idaho State University's Holt Arena. I found a coupon for the Grizzly and Wolf Discovery

206

Center. (I cut that out.) Then I found the page that listed all the area codes. Even for countries.

It was confusing. I entered 011, which I thought was the code for the U.S. And then, even though the phone book didn't say to do this, I entered 411, because that's the number for Information. And then I entered 8115 for Japan. And then I entered 411 again. I was so excited that my finger was very shaky. Then, the best thing started happening. I heard the phone ringing. Yay!

But then, call waiting beeped. At first I thought I would ignore it. Then I worried that it might be Nina calling about the volcano. I went ahead and hung up on Japan and answered the call coming in.

"Camille!" my father cheered. "How are you?"

"I'm okay," I said.

"I miss you," he said.

"I've heard that before," I said.

"It's the truth," he said. "I think about you all the time."

"Yeah," I said. "That's what happens when you leave people."

"Don't be that way, Camille. Everything is going to be okay. I'll be home soon."

Hearing him say that everything was going to be okay made me feel a little bit better.

"How soon is soon?" I asked, twisting the phone cord around my wrist.

"Two weeks," he said.

"I can't live with that," I said. Even though he didn't understand the full meaning of this, I pushed the 9 button on the phone. I decided that when people on the phone said things that I disagreed with, I'd push 9 for no.

"Don't do that, Camille. It's annoying."

"Really?" I asked, pressing the 9 button three more times.

"Camille, let's have a conversation," he said.

"I conversed all day at school already," I said. Plus, I had to save a lot of conversing for Sally.

"How was school?" he asked. "Are you still learning about the decimal point?"

I pushed the 9 button again. We were mostly dividing numbers now in math.

"Camille, stop that," he said, sounding extremely irritated. "I'm calling to see how you are. I want to make sure you're okay."

"I'm okay," I said, picking up a penny and balancing it on my nose.

"I love you," he said. "This wasn't my idea. But we'll work it out. Okay? And don't push any buttons!"

I put my finger on the 9 button, but I didn't push it.

"Okay," I said, taking the penny off of my nose. "I love you too."

When I hung the phone up, I felt halfway sad and halfway hopeful. It wasn't really anything that my dad said, it was because I realized what a great phone we had. It was brick red and had big, black buttons that lit up in the dark, and unlike some phones I'd used, it didn't have any annoying static. It also had caller ID.

Then my hopeful feeling went away, because the phone rang again, and when I answered it, I learned some horrible news.

"You have four minutes left on your calling card," said a woman with a robot voice. I quickly pressed 9 for no. Then I listened for more information. "Your call to Slovakia will end in three minutes."

I pushed the disconnect button over and over. What was happening? I hadn't called Slovakia. I didn't even have that calling card. Then I started reading the other country codes. I looked up Slovakia. It was 421. Had I pressed 421 instead of 411? Should I not have pressed 411? Then I started reading the instructions for my international calling card.

Turns out it was good for more countries than just Japan. Turns out that when I clicked over to take my dad's call, my calling card had called Slovakia without my permission. Turns out I only had three minutes left and there was no way to get my minutes back. Then I heard the dial tone, which meant that things were over with my calling card. I thought about all the quarters I'd saved and tried to not cry. I thought about what Mrs. Bratberg had told me when she'd given me my bills: "Don't spend it all in one place."

But I had spent it all in one place. I sat down on the floor and rocked a little bit. And hugged myself. I wanted to forget I'd ever heard that robot voice. I wanted to forget a lot of things.

CHAPTER 25

AND the loser is . . .

On Friday, when I went out to catch the bus, Polly was sitting on my front steps, waiting to walk up my driveway with me.

"Where's your science project?" she asked.

"Nina Hosack is bringing it," I said. I didn't even look at Polly. She should not have been on my steps. I hadn't invited her, so she was trespassing. And that was something that was against the law.

"Hannah's mom is going to drive ours to school. It

involves delicate Styrofoam balls," she said, bunching up her face and looking concerned.

I didn't want to talk about our science projects. Thinking about losing five thousand dollars made my whole body hurt, even my toes, which never hurt. Even when people accidentally stepped on them.

"Hey, is your dad on a trip?" Polly asked. "I haven't seen his pickup in a long time."

When Polly asked me this, I felt a pain sink into me. I didn't want to admit to anybody that my parents were separated. I wanted to pretend that everything was okay. And then I wanted everything to start being okay again.

"He's traveling," I said. "It's how he makes a living."

And I don't remember what Polly said after this. Because I was so supersad that I went to a place deep inside of my own head. I just kept thinking. And I thought so much that I lost track of time. One minute I was standing in my driveway listening to Polly. The next minute, my legs were walking my disconnected self through the school's front door.

Nina flagged down my head and my body right away. When I say "flagged down," I mean that she literally had an American flag that she was waving above her head as she called out my name. Watching my science partner act like a total idiot in a crowded area made my head and body reconnect themselves in a hurry.

"What's the deal?" I asked.

"I need to let you know that I didn't just build a regular volcano." As she talked, Nina looked over each of her shoulders to make sure that nobody was listening.

"What did you build?" I asked, looking over each of my shoulders too.

"A volcanic monument to our country," Nina said, placing her hand on her heart.

"I don't know what that is," I said. "But if it doesn't require batteries, then I want my five bucks back." Because I really missed having an emergency five dollars in my underwear drawer.

"It still uses a battery," she said. "It's like a volcano, except better. Instead of red lava, I made ours blue. And instead of a regular old brown earthlike-looking volcano, I made ours red and molded it in the shape of America. The volcano's cone is located over Missouri. And I filled the magma reservoir with the blue lava and white plastic stars. So when it erupts, it will be a tribute to our country. I brought a flag for each of us. During the eruption, I think we should sing 'God Bless America.' "

I wasn't sure how to react, so I raised my eyebrows and pressed my lips together. I raised my eyebrows to communicate to Nina that I was surprised by her level of creativity. I pressed my lips together to let her know that I wasn't sure if her idea was a good one or a bad one. Nina said the idea came to her when she was walking home from my house and every car that passed her had either an American flag flying from a window or a USA bumper sticker pasted to its back end.

"Why Missouri?" I asked, keeping my eyebrows lifted and lips tightened. "Do they have volcanoes there?"

"Not that I'm aware of," she said. "But it doesn't matter. It's symbolic. Missouri is in America's heartland. Got it?"

I got it. But I also got tired of communicating with Nina through my eyebrows, so I relaxed them. But I kept my lips tightened, because I'd just discovered that this helped me think. Staring at Nina, I noticed that she looked a little crazed. Her eyes were unfocused and she kept darting her gaze from the ceiling to the floor. Little drops of sweat beaded her upper lip.

"Are you running a temperature?" I asked.

"I'm just fired up," she said, grabbing on to one of my shoulders. "It's cool to be patriotic. We'll win the prize money for sure."

I hoped she was right. Then I took a step back. I had never seen Nina act crazy like this before. I was used to seeing her wimpy side.

"This is the first time I've ever seen you fired up," I said.

Nina smiled. "Do you know what I think it is?" she asked.

"What?" I asked. Because I was very curious about this.

"Fighting off that dog at your house boosted my self-esteem," she said.

That is not the way I remembered things happening when we dug up Muffin and Pinky showed up. But I didn't have the energy to disagree.

Nina moved toward me and grabbed my shoulder again. A wide grin broke across her face as she gently shook me.

"This is going to be so great," she said.

"I don't know," I said. "I'm not sure whether I know all of the words to 'God Bless America.' "

Nina let go of me and twirled one of her blond pigtails around her pointer finger. She was thinking about something. Sweat beads formed on her forehead and around her hairline. Then her face flashed with happiness and she let out a squeal.

"I've got it," she said. "You just hum and I'll sing." And then Nina handed me my very own flag and saluted me. "God bless America," she said as she flipped around the other way and ran down the hall.

When I got to class, everybody's projects were set up in plain view on their desks. Except for ours. Nina had draped a red sheet over our project so that nobody could see it. I sighed when I saw that five other groups had built volcanoes. Polly and Hannah had built the solar system using Styrofoam balls and wire. I thought their Mars looked just as big as their Jupiter, but because I'm not a rude person, I didn't say anything.

I couldn't tell what Tony Maboney and Boone Berry had made. All I could see on Tony's desk was a dead fish in a clear plastic box. The fish was smaller than my thumbnail. And it wasn't any color at all. It almost looked invisible, except for a thin, neon green line that ran through the center of its body.

When it came time to present the projects, Nina shot her hand up and asked if we could go last. Tony Maboney shot his hand up and said that he wanted to go last too. I didn't know what was so great about going last, but I decided to support my partner. Mr. Hawk said that because we'd asked first, we could go last.

Nina reacted by screaming, "Woot, woot!"

By the time we got to Tony Maboney's dead fish, I was bored out of my skull. Four out of the five volcanoes were duds. No eruption. Not even a little. Watching a volcano not erupt is about as exciting as watching a faucet not drip. Nina didn't seem to feel this way.

Every time a volcano was a dud, she had a hard time containing her happiness. She drummed her feet on the floor and shot me wicked-looking smiles. I started to wonder if Nina had somehow sabotaged the other projects. But when the fifth volcano did erupt, I just chalked up all the other duds as coincidences.

Tony and Boone stood in front of their desks and announced that they were going to perform a resurrection. When they said this, some of the churchgoing kids gasped. Mr. Hawk jumped up from behind his desk.

"We have frozen this fish," Tony said, "and now we're going to thaw it and bring it back to life."

Mr. Hawk sat back down. Tony and Boone didn't look very confident. Tony shoved both of his hands deep down into his front pockets. Both he and Boone were biting their lower lips. And when Boone opened up the plastic container, his hand trembled so badly that he almost dropped the lid.

"Freezing the fish is not easy," Boone explained as he scooped the fish up with a plastic spoon and moved it onto a paper plate. "You can't just pop it in the freezer. We have used a colorless, odorless chlorofluorocarbon to freeze this fish."

"Where did you get that?" Penny asked. "That sounds illegal!"

"No interrupting," Mr. Hawk said.

"My Uncle Rick got it for me," Boone said. "He's a high school chemistry teacher in Utah."

Penny frowned. She didn't look happy. But it didn't matter. Several of us in the class let out a series of "oohs." Even I did. If Tony and Boone had figured out how to bring a fish back to life, nobody else stood a chance of winning. I looked at Nina. She crossed her fingers on both hands and glared at the fish like it was pure evil.

When Tony plugged a navy blue hair dryer into an outlet, everybody sat on the edge of their seats.

"Thawing the fish is very difficult too," Boone said, flipping the hair dryer on to its lowest setting. "If the fish doesn't freeze fast enough, the fluid in its tissue will crystallize. If ice crystals form, they will act like daggers and knives, puncturing the fish's cells. This same thing could happen when it thaws."

A chorus of "oohs" floated through the room again. It was like we were watching a real scientist. Boone was using words that were so big, nobody would have been able to spell them. Gracie screamed when the fish's body twitched. Boone quickly shut the hair dryer off and lifted the paper plate over a bowl filled with water. He gently shook the plate until the fish slipped off and plopped into the water. Their fish still acted a little dead, like it had been only partially resurrected. But in a couple of seconds it zigged and zagged around the bowl. Boone dropped some food flakes into the water and his resurrected fish darted straight to the surface and gobbled them up.

Everybody clapped and stomped their feet. Tony and Boone took several bows in front of the class. They slapped each other a high five as they cleaned up their project.

"Nina and Camille," Mr. Hawk said, "are you ready?"

"Yes, sir!" Nina said.

Nina stood beside her desk and took hold of two of the red sheet's corners.

"Feast your eyes on this!" she said, trying to rip the sheet off the volcano in one, dramatic pull. But it didn't quite work out the way she wanted. The sheet caught on something.

"Feast your eyes on this!" she repeated, tugging the sheet so hard that the volcano flipped right off her desk and into the lap of Zoey Combs. Blue lava oozed out of the volcano's cone and onto Zoey. Unfortunately for Zoey, she was wearing a knee-high skirt and no tights. She had a lot of exposed skin.

"Ahhh!" Zoey yelled, flipping our volcano onto the floor. "It's gooey!"

I didn't react. Just like Tony and Boone's fish before it was resurrected, I was perfectly still. Nina dove after our volcano and dropped her flag on the floor.

Tony jumped to his feet. "You've got to burn that flag now," he said. "When you drop an American flag on the ground you have to burn it. It's in the Constitution."

"It's not in the Constitution," Mr. Hawk said, walking toward Zoey with a wad of paper towels in his hand.

"This stings! What's in it? Is it acid?" Zoey hollered, furiously wiping the lava off her.

"I think the stars are poking you," I said.

"They are! They are! The stars are poking me!"

Nina tried to scoop the lava from the floor back into the volcano's center. She scooped and scooped. If I hadn't known any better, I would've thought Nina was a professional lava scooper, competing in the Lava-Scooping Olympics. Blue lava stuck to Nina's red shirt in many interesting patterns. And the more she scooped, the more she sweated. Beads of sweat dropped off her forehead and onto her shirt, staining the fabric a deeper red. And circles began to grow near her armpits—wet, dark, and stinky ones.

"Help me!" Nina yelled as she struggled to set the volcano back on top of her desk.

I took ahold of one end of the volcano and slid it onto her desk. But I pushed too hard and the volcano slid off the desk again. The spilled lava had made everything very slippery. Every time we moved, our shoes squeaked. When the volcano slipped this time, I decided to be the one to dive after it. I should have stuck to being a dingo and sat down in the corner and admired myself. But I felt obligated to do something more.

I jumped in the general direction that it was heading, but I tripped over Nina's fallen flag. The last thing

I saw before my head hit the fishbowl was the expression of terror and despair on Boone Berry's face. You might think that knocking a fishbowl onto the floor with your head would be terribly painful. But it's not. Not when you have five pounds of hair to soften the blow.

CHAPTER 26

MELTDOWN

When my head smashed into the fishbowl and I knocked it onto the floor, it was like a miracle had happened. Because the glass didn't break. It landed right-side up and bounced a little. But then the miracle ended and the bowl tipped over onto its side and cracked open. Water gushed everywhere, and the resurrected fish floated onto the floor. It flopped on top of several shards of broken glass.

"Save it!" Tony yelled.

Boone scooped the fish up with the plastic spoon and dumped it into a cup filled with water.

"Is it okay?" Zoey gushed, grabbing at her heart.

"She killed it," Tony yelled. "Camille McPhee's big hippo head killed our fish."

"Tony," snapped Mr. Hawk.

I could feel tears forming in my eyes.

"I didn't mean to," I said. "I slipped."

"Fish killer!" Tony yelled. "You should travel on a motorized scooter. There's no telling when you'll fall again. Mrs. Zirklezack is nuts to put you on top of a bucket."

This made me very sad. I looked down at the sloppy floor. I already felt a lot of pressure about standing on my bucket. Now it was worse.

"It's okay," Boone said. "It's not the end of the world. I mean, it is the end of the world for our fish, but it's okay."

I had blue lava smeared all over my arms. I was a mess.

"Do you want me to mop it up?" I asked Mr. Hawk.

"That's all right, Camille. Why don't you girls go visit Mrs. Blaze."

Zoey let out a frightened squeak. Mrs. Blaze was the school nurse. She had a reputation for putting stinging medicine on open cuts and knocking people's knees with a hammer. I'd visited her a bunch of times. But never with a group. We walked down the hallway and stood outside Mrs. Blaze's door. Pictures of healthy things were taped on it. Apples. A toothbrush. A tall glass of milk. And a clown wearing a Band-Aid on its cheek.

"That clown looks creepy," Zoey said. "Like it's been in a fight with another clown."

Mrs. Blaze heard us talking and opened the door.

"Did somebody say they'd been in a fight?" Mrs. Blaze asked. She reached out toward us and told us to come inside. She had gray hair and gray eyes and she was also wearing gray pants. And to look official, she had on a white doctor's coat.

"Camille," she said. "How are you? I haven't seen you since your big sugar crash last spring."

She rubbed my shoulder with concern.

"Actually," I said, "the last time I saw you was in December. Because I ran into problems cutting out my snowflake."

"Right," she said. "How is your finger?"

I lifted it up and looked at it. Then I bent it four times.

"Normal," I said.

"It looks like you girls have had an accident," Mrs. Blaze said.

"Yes! My skin burns!" Zoey interrupted. "I might

need to go to the emergency room and take a special bath!"

"I doubt it," Nina said. "I used nontoxic ingredients for the volcano. Because I have very sensitive skin."

"That's true," I added. "When she washes, she uses a special bar of soap."

"Okay. Okay," Mrs. Blaze said. "Tell me what happened."

I let Nina describe the situation. She was still very proud of her volcano. Even though it was basically junk now.

"That's a very dramatic science fair," Mrs. Blaze said. She wrung out a bunch of washcloths and handed them to us.

"Science is disgusting," Zoey said, wiping the lava off her legs.

Zoey and Gracie had built a mold terrarium. They'd stuck a bunch of different foods in a glass jar and let it rot. They wanted to show off all the different types and colors of mold. Their lemon grew a blue-green powder. Their strawberries sprouted a gray fuzz. And their bread produced mold that looked very white and puffy. So I wasn't surprised that Zoey thought science was disgusting. Because not only was her project gross, it was also a real bummer.

"Science can be very interesting," Mrs. Blaze said. "That was my college major."

"Really?" Nina asked.

"Yes," Mrs. Blaze said. "I studied the nitty-gritty truth about how things operate. In plants. And animals. And people. I loved it!"

"I think I want to be a scientist!" Nina said.

I looked at Nina like she was sort of crazy. Because from what I knew of her, she wasn't ready for the nitty or the gritty.

"But Mrs. Blaze, we lost," I said.

"What did you lose?" Mrs. Blaze asked.

"The science fair," I said. "And there was a cash prize. Also, I killed that fish. I feel very terrible."

I handed her my washcloth and she threw it in a hamper.

"I know. That's too bad," Mrs. Blaze said. "Can I give you some advice?"

"Okay," I said. Because I trusted Mrs. Blaze. She wore a neat bun *and* had a jar filled with tongue depressors. I was sure what she was about to tell me would be very inspiring.

"Don't worry about this too much. Because one day you're going to look back on it and laugh," she said.

She smiled at me and handed me a scratch-'n'-sniff sticker with a bunch of grapes on it. I thought that was pretty bad advice. Because, even if I did feel like it one day, laughing at a dead fish seemed like a mean thing to do. I scratched my sticker, but the smell wasn't very strong. Nina got a blueberry one that gave off a very powerful stink. And Zoey got a banana that smelled so much like a real banana that it made my stomach grumble.

"Don't be afraid to come back and visit," Mrs. Blaze said.

"Okay!" Nina said. She sounded very thrilled and it bugged me.

"Stickers are for babies," Zoey said. But I saw her sniffing hers anyway.

Every second of that day, all I could think about was how my head had led to the death of an exceptional fish. My mind was like a laser beam. Even when I walked through my front door.

"Camille!" my mother cheered when I came home. For some reason, my sadness was turning into anger. It ticked me off that my mother sounded so happy. Why was she so happy? What was there to be happy about? We had a big Visa bill. She and my father were separated. Her only child, me, obviously wasn't doing too well, because I had just taken the life of a resurrected fish. Plus, I'd dug up my dead cat to try to win the science fair. And I was being forced to play the part of an unwanted cat while standing on a wobbly, elevated surface. Not to mention my calling-card disaster. Could my life get any worse?

My mother didn't even ask me about my day. Instead, she handed me a DVD.

"I rented us a movie," she said. "It's called *The World's Deadliest Swarms.*"

I handed the DVD back to her.

"I've got homework," I said, stomping down the hall. I hadn't been able to finish my spelling at school, due to the fact that I'd been covered in lava and had to visit Mrs. Blaze.

"But it's Friday," she said.

I had forgotten that it was Friday. This was pretty good news. And to be honest, a program called *The World's Deadliest Swarms* sounded interesting. I liked education best when it was about dangerous and gross animals.

After we talked, my mom flew out the door. She had a kickboxing class to teach. I was surprised that people wanted to go to the gym and work out on Friday nights. But my mother said that she had a core group of followers. She said they were addicted to her Friday-night Turbo Kick It & Bam It class. I just didn't get that.

While my mom was gone, I tried to call Aunt Stella. But I just got her machine. So I left a message.

"It's Camille. I was hoping we could talk about school, because science isn't going so great for me. Did you ever build anything for a science fair? I had a partner. So I didn't get to make exactly what

I wanted. Hey, Aunt Stella, did you know that it's possible to freeze a fish and resurrect it? Well, it is. Science is teaching me a lot of new things. Talk later. Hey, I love you."

After I left my message, I moved the couch and coffee table so we could watch the movie on the floor. I kept hoping that my dad would call so that I could talk to him again. I had made a promise to myself that I would have a conversation with him this time and that I wouldn't press the 9 button. But the phone never rang.

When my mom got back, she hopped through the front door dripping with sweat. Once she was cleaned off, she popped the disc into the DVD player.

"It's a reenactment of the ten worst swarms of the century," my mother said energetically, plopping herself down beside me on the floor.

I was impressed that my mother had rented this film. Bugs weren't really her thing. Anytime she came across something buglike in our house, she always squished it with a tissue and flushed it down the toilet. She was also an expert fly and mosquito swatter. A lot of times she struck them down with a magazine in midair.

My dad always caught bugs with his bare hands and then took them outside and let them go. He said he was liberating them. My mother didn't see it that way.

She said she was helping them rest in peace. I missed my dad.

"I almost forgot," she said, hopping back up and running into the kitchen.

My mother brought out some snacks and set them down on the floor between us.

"They're low-sodium soy nuts," she said, patting me on the back.

"What about popcorn?" I asked.

"You don't want to stuff yourself with carbohydrates and sodium," she said, pinching my cheek. "Not at this time of night."

Then my mother proudly put the soy nuts in front of me.

"I only got us one ice water. We'll need more hydration than that," she said, smacking the heel of her hand to her forehead. She sprang off the floor and dashed to the kitchen.

Everything inside of me felt bad. I was sure that if a doctor had unzipped my skin, he would have seen all the anger and sadness stuck near my heart. I breathed hard. And thought of the many things I wanted to yell. *Let me eat popcorn! I don't care about stinking carbohydrates. Or sodium. I'm ten! When you're ten, you eat carbohydrates and sodium. Even when it's late. And you don't worry about hydration. EVER!* But I didn't yell any of these things. Instead, I reached out and knocked the bowl of soy nuts over. Then I poured the glass of ice water on them and smeared them around.

When my mother came back, she stepped right in the mess, soaking both of her socks.

"What happened?" she asked. "Our new carpet!"

But before I could answer, she flew down the hall to get a towel. Then, with a lot of enthusiasm, she cleaned up the mess and replaced both the soy nuts and the water.

Three tears rolled down my cheeks. I counted them. Two tears came from my right eye and one from my left. It was so dark that my mother didn't notice that I was crying.

Watching the deadliest swarms didn't cheer me up at all. It just showed how unfair life was all over the planet. In nine of the cases, everybody lived and was okay, even a boy who fell into a den of rattlesnakes. Even a man who was stung by more than a hundred jellyfish. But a little girl's mother was killed by a swarm of bees. They weren't even killer bees. They were regular old honeybees.

"This is horrifying!" my mother said.

I watched her lift handful after handful of soy nuts to her mouth. Then I turned back to the television. In the reenactment, the mother wrapped her own body around the girl to keep her from getting stung. The mother held her really close and whispered in her ear.

She told her that they were going to be okay. And I believed her. But when the paramedics showed up, they announced that the girl's mother was dead. I felt horrible. I cried three more tears. *How awful and unfair*, I thought, *to promise someone that there was hope when nobody really knew for sure.*

I hid my tears and told my mom that I thought that was a lousy trick, telling the girl everything was going to be okay. "They were getting stung by a thousand crazy bees!" I said.

"It wasn't a trick," my mother said, rubbing my back. "I bet the mother wanted everything to be okay so badly that she really believed it would be. That's not lying. It's how our brains work."

When I started thinking about how my own brain might be playing tricks on me, I got so upset that I decided to go straight to bed.

Later that night, I heard my mother answer the phone. By the tone of her voice, I could tell it was my father. I now knew that I could no longer believe everything my father said. When he told me that everything was going to be okay, what he really meant was that his brain *hoped* that everything was going to be okay. There's a huge difference.

"Her play is next week. I think you should come," she said. "No, this doesn't mean that anything has changed. You can sleep on the couch."

Shortly after she told my father that nothing had changed and he could sleep on the couch, she hung up the phone. She didn't slam it down. She just hung it up. When I heard the click of the phone being placed back in the handset, something clicked inside me too. Somewhere deep inside I heard a voice say, *Don't worry. Everything is going to be okay.*

But I couldn't trust my own brain anymore. I turned my face into my pillow and let out deep sobs. When it got hard to breathe, I turned my head to the side and gasped and coughed and sucked in fresh air. I was shaking and my hair was sticking in clumps to my wet face. I cried as quietly as I could for a long time.

I bet after her father died, Polly cried like this all of the time. I bet when her brain told her that everything was going to be okay, she was smart enough to know that her brain might be a liar.

That night it was hard to stop crying. I missed my father. I missed Sally. I missed my three cats. I missed the resurrected fish, even though I'd barely gotten to know it. I missed the twenty-two minutes I'd lost on my international calling card, too.

I missed so many things that I started running out of stuff to miss and I had to get out an old photo album to jog my memory. I'm glad I did that, because it reminded me of a lot of things I didn't have anymore.

CHAPTER 27

PERSONAl GROWTh

My weekend wasn't good. I missed Aunt Stella's first phone call because I was outside with my mother helping her fertilize flowers that hadn't even bloomed yet. And I missed Aunt Stella's second phone call because I was in the bathtub removing mud from myself. But I listened to her message after I got dry.

"Camille, I did enter a science fair once. But science was never my favorite subject. My project

involved magnets, and I can't remember it exactly. By the way, I'm very curious to know what's going on with that play of yours."

But by the time I got her message, my skin was shriveled up like a raisin and I didn't have the energy to call her back. I just pretended like something was in my eye a lot, so my mom wouldn't notice I was crying.

By Monday, I was very ready to get on my school bus and forget about my problems and start acting like a dingo again. I didn't realize that all that thinking and crying and bathing had changed me a little bit. But that day, at the bus stop, something very important happened. And I didn't even mean for it to happen. In fact, until it did happen, I thought I was having a regular day.

Manny and Danny skipped small stones across the road. Polly no longer stood in line with us. She stood on the other side of my mailbox. I think she liked having a barrier between her and Manny and Danny.

Manny and Danny tossed some rocks at the ground by Polly's feet, hitting her shoes.

"Dance for us, Polly," Danny said. He and Manny were nudging each other with their elbows and laughing. They were laughing so hard they were snorting.

I don't know if I had extra anger inside of me because my parents were still on a break. Or maybe I felt this way because I'd watched that DVD about deadly swarms. All I know is that when I saw tears in Polly's eyes, it reminded me that her father was gone—forever. And Manny and Danny didn't seem to understand what this meant. It's like they didn't even care. Someone had to do something. Enough was enough.

"No more pushing Polly around," I said, stomping my foot on the ground. "I've talked to my dad about this situation, and he's not happy."

"But your dad's not here, is he?" Danny asked in a snotty voice.

"No, not at the moment," I said, standing my ground. "But I'll tell him. I'll tell him every awful thing you two are doing and when he gets back he'll come and talk to you."

Manny put his rocks down. But Danny didn't.

Danny stared at me hard, and I stared right back at him. He had a lot more freckles than I realized. Especially on his nose. We stared and we stared. After a while, my eyeballs felt dry and I had to blink. This bugged me, because I knew that blinking was a sign of weakness. And I didn't feel weak. My eyeballs just got dry. Then I started talking, and I was surprised by how tough I sounded.

"Do you feel lucky, Danny?" I asked, walking toward him. I drew a line in the dirt with the toe of my sneaker. "From now on, you stay there and we stay here. And no chucking rocks or hocking loogies over it. This is our area. Got it?" I said firmly.

"What if I don't?" Danny said with a smirk.

I walked up to the line so both of my toes were right on the edge. "Go ahead, Danny," I said, setting my cooler down in the dirt. "Make my day."

Danny tossed his rocks into the road and shot me a dirty look. Polly walked over and stood behind me.

"That's the nicest thing anyone has done for me in a long time," she said, looking at the ground. "I like Clint Eastwood too."

"Get used to it," I said, picking my cooler back up. "This is the brand-new Camille McPhee." I wasn't sure what she meant about Clint Eastwood. I didn't know who the heck he was. But that day, when crossing the road to get on the bus, I slapped the bumper with my hand and stuck my tongue out at it and said, "Meet the brand-new Camille McPhee!"

Polly laughed. Mrs. Spittle said I wasn't allowed to touch the bus ever again. She said it was school policy. Especially for me. She was firm on that.

On the bus, Polly told me all about Clint Eastwood. She said that he was a pretty famous actor who, when he was younger, liked to play cowboys and police officers. Polly said that he also starred in a movie with an orangutan named Clyde. But that was a while ago. She also thought the orangutan might have been mistreated on the movie set, and that didn't surprise me, because I already knew that monkeys' lives were pretty unfair. Then, because Polly knew so much about Clint Eastwood, I asked her if she knew anything about dingoes. She did.

She said that in Australia, dingoes weren't popular because they ate helpless sheep. She'd also heard of cases where dingoes had eaten helpless babies. Not sheep babies. Human babies!

"They're a real nuisance, and if they're not on a reserve or a national park, people are allowed to shoot them," she said.

This really bummed me out. I was under the impression that dingoes were proud, lovely animals. Polly made them sound almost as bad as brown tree snakes. After learning this, I wondered if it was time to part ways with my dingo side. Because what did I really have in common with a dingo?

Other than learning about Clint Eastwood and dingoes, the bus ride was uneventful. When I got to school, it turned out that Tony was sick. That made me happy. And Nina smiled at me. I liked that. And the science contest winner couldn't be announced until tomorrow, because the judge had to pass a kidney stone first. And Polly slipped me a note.

You have the prettiest hair in the school.

I folded the note up and stuffed it in my cooler next to my turkey sandwich. Then Mr. Hawk said something that caught my attention *and* ruined my day.

"I have a surprise. Sally Zook sent me a letter from Japan," he said. "She wanted me to read it to the class."

For a second, I didn't believe that he had a letter from Sally Zook. But then he pulled it out and I saw it with my own two eyes. Then I thought maybe there were two Sally Zooks in the world. But I didn't think that for very long. Because Sally was so special, I knew there could only be one of her.

And so Mr. Hawk read Sally's letter about how great Japan was and all the monkeys she'd seen. I was very angry that my very good friend would send Mr. Hawk a letter, our whole class a letter, before she wrote to me. And where was my bathrobe? I bet she made up kimonos. I was so upset that when school was over, I walked to the paper map of the world at the back of the classroom. I searched until I found Japan. It looked like a lousy, lime green pinto bean. I took out the piece of gum I'd been chewing all afternoon and stuck it to Japan. That's what I thought of Japan. That's what I thought of Sally Zook.

Sadly, my gum had too much spit on it, and it slid off the map and landed on the floor. Japan! Sally! I hoped I never heard anything about either one of them again.

CHAPTER 28

hope

I went home extremely ticked off at the world. But one good thing about being me was that Camille McPhee was the kind of mammal who was born with the power to bounce back.

Once, my neighbor's ferret, Denise II, jumped on my back and sank her teeth into me. My father had to grab Denise II by the scruff of her neck and pull her off me. For some reason, that ferret went totally nuts for two minutes. Nobody knew why. Both my dad and I got pretty scratched up. But I didn't go around the rest of my life hating ferrets named Denise. I forgave her and moved on.

I didn't even have to be conscious for my ability to bounce back to work. I could go to sleep feeling sour and upset, and I could wake up feeling sweet and okay. For me, bouncing back didn't seem to take much effort. When I woke the next day, the world was still an unfair bomb of stink, but I felt a little bit better about this. I hoped that by Friday, the day of our first performance, I would still feel this way. In front of my mom and dad, I wanted to be the best and most energetic cat that I could possibly be. And I wanted to stay upright on my bucket, even if I did drown. I cared about the other performances, too. The one for the first through third graders. And the one for the general public. But out of the three, the parents' performance was the one that worried me the most.

The next morning, my laser-beam mind had a new focus. I wanted to know if Polly's cat ate tuna fish and licked up her tears. Because all three of my cats had been tuna-fish eaters and tear lickers. And I wondered if all cats were like that. Or just my cats. But I didn't know how to bring it up naturally. A lot of times, when I was stuck like this, I just went ahead and brought it up anyway, even if it was unnatural.

Polly was waiting for me on my front steps again. When I opened my door, I was surprised to see her hair. It was still blond, but it was a lot shorter. And it looked thick. All its stringiness had vanished.

"I like your hair," I said. "It looks completely different."

"Thanks," she said. She reached up and touched it.

"It really looks fantastic," I said. I mean, I was surprised by such a drastic change. Polly had never been drastic before.

"I hadn't cut it in three years," she said.

I slapped my knee. "Wow! Were you going for a record?"

Once, I went for a record. I kicked my legs back and forth in the air like superpowered scissors for as long as I could. My record was one minute. Then I lost my form.

"No," Polly said. "Not a record. After my dad died I didn't want to cut my hair."

I sat down next to Polly. I didn't know what to say. Luckily, she kept talking.

"After I understood that he was gone, I wanted to keep everything he'd touched: his clothes, cans of soup, even my hair."

This seemed very sad. I didn't ask her any questions about it. But it did make me realize that I shouldn't go around judging people who have stringy hair, because maybe they have a very good reason for having hair like that.

"I think your hair looks super," I said.

"My mom says that change is good." She ran her fingers through her bob.

"My mom says that too," I said. "But it usually means that she wants to buy something new."

Polly smiled at me like she was able to read my mind, like she understood the deeper meaning of what I'd said. We walked to the bus stop and stood by ourselves. Both Manny and Danny had come down with mono. I wasn't too surprised. They were always drinking out of other people's soda cans and milk cartons. And a couple of times, accepting a stupid dare, they'd licked the monkey bars. I'd seen them do it. Twice, they'd wiped their tongues over the shiny metal bars and then stuck them out for everybody to see. I thought if you were dumb enough to do that, catching mono was the least of your problems.

I looked at Polly, and her new bob. I looked at the sky. I looked at my shoes. I looked back at the sky. I looked at Polly's shoes. I adjusted my socks. I suggested that Polly adjust her socks too. Then I blurted it out. "What's your cat's name?"

I thought the question would roll off my tongue like an ordinary question. But for some reason, I didn't use my regular voice. I used a loud voice. And for some other reason, I aimed my hand at her like my finger was a gun.

Polly didn't notice.

"Orca," she said. "My dad named her Orca because she's a mix of black and white. *Orcinus orca* is the scientific name for killer whales. They're black and white too."

"Does Orca eat tuna fish?" I asked, trying to sound more normal.

"No. They mainly eat salmon, shrimp, herring, and squid. But sometimes they'll eat a seal, dophin, or walrus."

For one second my brain got confused and I tried to picture a cat eating a walrus. I thought Polly's walrus-eating cat was the weirdest animal in the galaxy. Then I realized that Polly was talking about killer whales.

"I don't mean killer whales. I mean your cat."

"Oh, Orca loves tuna fish," she said, nodding.

"The first cat I ever had used to lick my face," I said, trying to be tactful. I didn't want to use the word *tears,* because I didn't want to make Polly sad or embarrass her.

"Sometimes when my eyes watered, she would lick up the liquid around my eyes," I said, trying to pitch it so it sounded like a question. "Maybe she liked the salt."

"Orca is a great licker," Polly said, bouncing around like a spring. "She is the best and kindest and most thoughtful cat on the planet. Maybe after school you can hang out with us."

Polly explained to me that Orca only had one and a half ears because she had been involved in a big fight with a raccoon. Her father had called the fight an unfortunate brouhaha. Now Orca was strictly an indoor cat. Polly wanted to make sure that I knew this, so I didn't accidentally let Orca outside.

"The whole time I've had her, she's never been outside," Polly said.

That didn't make total sense to me, because she'd just told me that her cat had fought a raccoon. But then I thought maybe the raccoon had gotten in Polly's house or something. Maybe it had climbed inside through her chimney.

"I get it," I said. "I won't let your cat escape."

Orca sounded like a perfectly good friend for Polly. Too bad about that chimney raccoon biting off her ear. I hated that unfair things could happen to cats, too.

When I got to school, my head felt disconnected from my body again. Today the results for the science fair were announced. I spent a lot of time looking down at my loafers. There were several people who I wanted to avoid making eye contact with. Mr. Hawk, Boone, Tony, Nina, Zoey, and the rest of my class were at the top of that list. No one had really gotten over the fish.

When I walked into the classroom, I noticed a blue

ribbon and first-place certificate on top of Tony's desk. Nina's desk had a certificate for an honorable mention. Both of our names were on it. I sighed. Then I spotted a wooden cross and some daisies on the floor right where the resurrected fish had died. Someone had even left a card with FOR THE FISH printed on the pink envelope.

I sat at my desk. There was a note on it. When I unfolded the note, I knew it was from Tony. It had a picture of a stick figure with a big head standing on top of a bucket. And it had an arrow and a picture of the stick figure landing on its head. I understood exactly what he was saying. I folded the note back up. And decided to eat an apple. So I opened up my cooler. After I took a big crunchy bite, I felt a hand on my shoulder. I figured it was Mr. Hawk, but when I turned around to look at him, I saw that it was actually Boone. I bit my apple a second time.

"I want you to know that there's no hard feelings," Boone said.

"That's nice of you," I mumbled. Because I'd been taught good manners, I decided not to take another bite of my apple just yet.

"Tony had no right to call you a fish killer," he said.

"I didn't exactly help it stay alive," I answered.

"I guess. But what I mean to say is that our fish was going to die anyway. The other twenty fish we resurrected all died within the hour. That's why we wanted to go last. We could only bring it back to life temporarily."

When Boone said this, my ears started to get hot. I couldn't believe that they'd let me feel so rotten all weekend.

"That's crazy!" I said.

"I know. We were planning on switching that fish with another fish. Our project involved some cheating," he said.

I slapped my desk.

"Your project was all cheating!" I said.

"I'm sorry," he said.

But I didn't think that was enough.

"You've got to tell the class!" I said, setting my apple down on my desk. "They've built a memorial. They think I'm a killer! Plus, I'm getting hate mail." I showed him the note and tapped my finger by the picture of the stick figure landing on its head.

Boone looked like he was in pain. "I'm sorry, but I can't," he said. "I promised Tony."

"Tony's not the boss of your body," I snapped. After I said this, I wished I'd said something more mature. I sounded like I was in second grade or something.

"Actually, Tony's dad is the boss of my dad," he said, putting his hand back on my shoulder. "He owns the farm where my dad works. I don't want to cause any problems for him. You see how mean Tony is. Well, the apple doesn't fall far from the tree."

I looked out the window. The sun pushed its light through the glass, warming my face even more.

"But that's not fair," I said, poking him in his chest. (Boone had a very hard chest. He must've spent a lot of time lifting things that were heavy.)

"Tell me about it," Boone said. He backed up so my finger couldn't reach him. "Tony got really mad when I didn't take his side about Gracie's grizzly-bear picture. I'm sorry."

"But Gracie's grizzly-bear picture wasn't even a big deal," I said. "This is."

"Don't worry, Camille," Boone said. "People will get over it."

After Boone said this, he went to his desk. I made eye contact with him several times throughout the day, trying to encourage him to make a speech to the class. But he didn't.

He just sat there and pretended to learn.

I knew he was wrong. Fourth graders didn't get over things. They remembered every screwup and held it against you. I knew, because I was a fourth grader!

All day long, I kept looking out the window. I watched clouds wander across the sky. I felt their shadows block the sun and creep over me. It was just like life. Because even a pretty sky has dark moments. I didn't want this to be true. But it was. I sat at my desk. Sometimes soaking in sun. Sometimes feeling the chill of shade. I couldn't believe that I was going to have to spend the rest of my life living in this gigantic unfair world.

During science, Mr. Hawk lectured on the bones of the body. After the fibula, tibia, femur, ribs, radius, ulna, scapula, clavicle, and vertebrae, he finally got to the head. When Mr. Hawk said the word *cranium,* Tony leaned forward and whispered, "Your cranium puts fish in mortal danger. Your cranium can't stay balanced on a bucket."

Knowing that Tony had killed twenty fish, and that I'd only killed one—and the one I killed was going to die anyway—made me furious. Soon, all the evil things I could do to Tony began to parade through my mind. I could put a dead trout on his doorstep every day for a year. No, I could slip a dead squid in his mailbox and let it rot. No, I could buy all sorts of fish guts and leave them out in the sun for a while and then hide them in his desk on a Friday. He'd be very surprised on Monday. But I realized that was actually a bad idea, because the stink would affect me too. And people I liked.

Before I knew it, school was over. When I got off the bus, Polly asked me if I wanted to come over to meet Orca.

"Okay," I said.

"Shouldn't you ask your mom?" Polly asked.

"She's teaching an advanced ball class. She won't be home for another thirty minutes."

Polly stopped walking and spun around. She did this so quickly that her blond bob whipped around and slapped her in the face.

"Your mom teaches aerobics and juggles?" she asked.

"No," I said. "Ball work is a type of aerobics class. It involves an inflatable ball."

Polly started laughing and then spun back around and continued walking home. Polly was funny. I sort of liked spending time with her. I also liked the idea of meeting her cat. Then I thought of a gift that I wanted to give her cat.

"I need to get something," I said. "I'll be right there!"

CHAPTER 29

ORCA?

Aunt Stella told me that when a baby is born in a hospital, one of the first things that the nurses do is fasten a name bracelet around the baby's leg. The nurses do this because they've birthed enough babies to know that when they're born, a lot of babies look the same—blotchy, pudgy, and pink. Nobody wants the babies to get mixed up. It's unusual, but sometimes one baby is mistaken for another baby and people take the wrong baby home. Sometimes it is fixed right away. But sometimes the people raise the wrong babies for a long time. Sometimes they grow up and nobody ever figures it out.

When I went to Polly's house, I wasn't thinking about babies or hospitals or mix-ups. I was just looking forward to meeting her cat. Standing on Polly's front steps, I noticed that her doorbell was broken. I knew this because right where I expected the doorbell to be, there were a red wire and a white wire sticking out of a hole.

Since there wasn't a sign telling me what to do with the wires, I figured I was supposed to touch the white and red wires together to make a ringing sound. But when I carefully pressed the tips of the wires together, instead of making a chiming noise or a ding-dong sound, the two wires started sparking. I yelled. Polly came to the door. I thought that this was a very dangerous doorbell system, but it worked.

"Here's a can of tuna fish," I said, handing the round tin to Polly.

"That was very nice of you," she said. Polly led me by the hand to her bedroom.

"Orca is in the closet," she said. "She likes to nap on top of my sweaters."

"My cat Checkers used to do that too," I said. "She especially liked my cotton-wool blends."

"So does Orca!" Polly cheered. "But she absolutely avoids polyester."

I nodded and smiled. Checkers felt that way about polyester too. Polly tossed a feather that was attached to a string into her closet. She slowly dragged the feather toward her.

"This always gets her," she said, kneeling down.

I thought it was too bad that Checkers had disappeared, because she and Orca liked the exact same things. I was sure that our two cats could have been best friends.

"She's wiggling her butt," Polly said. "She's getting ready to pounce."

I understood what Polly was saying. All three of my cats liked wiggling their butts before they pounced. When Orca leapt out of the closet, it was almost like I was watching Checkers. Their methods for lunging were very similar and they made the exact same thumping noise when they hit the carpet. While attacking the feather, Orca arched her back and bared her claws exactly how Checker used to. And the yin-yang pattern of black and white that decorated Orca's face looked identical to Checker's yin-yang pattern. Even their eyes were the same shade of green. They meowed the same and licked the same. Except for Checkers having two perfect pointy ears, and Orca only one and a half, they looked like twins. I thought this was quite a coincidence.

"How long have you had her?" I asked.

"About three years," she said, rubbing Orca's soft white belly.

I began to pet Orca too. And when I did, when I felt how she felt exactly like Checkers, a lightbulb went off in my head.

"Where did you buy her?" I asked, scratching behind her good ear.

"We didn't. We found her up a tree."

When Polly said this, it made me remember that Checkers had been an excellent climber. A lot of times, she'd scamper up a tree so high that we were afraid we'd have to call the fire department. Luckily, Checkers was good at sizing up limbs, and she always figured a way back down.

"Actually," Polly said, "my dad found her. Remember what I told you about her ear? Well, he was driving home from work and he ran over a raccoon. When he stopped to see if there was anything he could do, he noticed Orca stuck in a tree. My dad thought that the raccoon and Orca had been in a big fight. He thought that by running over the raccoon, he'd saved Orca's life."

I gathered Orca up in my arms and listened to her purr. She sounded a lot like my mother's Chevy. This was not Orca. Even though this cat smelled like Polly's sweaters, I still knew that underneath the smell, this was Checkers. I was absolutely sure.

"She was all scraped up. We took her to our vet."

"What if Orca belonged to somebody?" I asked. "Wasn't she wearing a collar?"

I couldn't believe this. My first very good friend had run off to Japan and never written me and now my second very good friend had stolen my cat.

"Actually, she did have an owner," Polly said, frowning. "My dad was planning to call the owner, but then he was in the accident."

When Polly said the word *accident*, I could see her eyes beginning to water. She took a deep breath and continued.

"A couple of weeks after his funeral, my mom finally called the owner. But I guess they didn't really like the cat. Because my mom said that the owner said we could keep her."

"Well, that doesn't sound right," I said. "Maybe your mom just said that so you wouldn't feel bad about stealing somebody else's cat." After I said this, I wondered if maybe I shouldn't have. But sometimes my mouth moved faster than the part of my brain that thought about what my mouth would say.

"That's an awful thing to say, Camille. You're calling my mom a liar. And a thief."

"I didn't mean that. I'm sorry. I've got to go." I picked up my cooler and ran out of her room and out of her house. She stood on her porch cradling Checkers/

Orca in her arms and watching me run. When I got halfway down her driveway I turned around and yelled, "Polly, you stole my cat!"

"What are you talking about?" she asked.

"Your cat Orca is really my cat Checkers," I said.

"You're wrong," she said.

"No, I'm not. And I didn't think you were the kind of person who would steal my cat."

Polly went inside and slammed her door. I wished I could have slammed a door too. But I was surrounded completely by air. This was all very terrible. I thought about how sad I was when Checkers disappeared. Then I thought of all those wasted minutes I'd spent looking for her. It was just like my calling card. Because nobody was going to be able to give me back those minutes either. I felt very mad. Before I went inside my house, I stopped for a moment in the garage. I peeled a banana and ate it, hoping it would make me feel better. I wondered if what Polly said was true. Would my mother or father have told Polly's mom that she could keep my cat? It seemed impossible. Life couldn't be that unfair. Could it?

After thinking about which one of my parents could have possibly given Checkers away, I became convinced that it had been my mother. Checkers wasn't perfect and had vomited a time or two on one of her favorite wool rugs. The first time this happened, my mother had yelled, "I'm so mad I could spit!" But she didn't. She bit her cheek and cleaned it up.

"Hair balls happen," my father had said.

And I agreed. Even if a cat does toss its cookies, it's not doing it on purpose. That's not a good enough reason to give it away. She should have known that! Then, for the umpteenth time, I sighed. I sighed because I knew what my future held.

In addition to being an unlucky cat owner, a cat digger-upper, a science-fair loser, a fish killer, a drowned cat (aka a feline with bad kismet), I also knew that I would have to be a mother confronter. I had to take a stand. For me. For Checkers. And for all the other unfortunate, nameless victims of mix-ups and switcheroos. I picked up my cooler and swung open the door.

CHAPTER 30

COMMUNICATION

There was no backing down. I had to be brave. To ensure that I would follow through with my confrontation, the first thing I did when I walked through the door was yell, "I've got a question!"

To my surprise, the voice that yelled back was not my mother's.

"Will I need an encyclopedia?" my father asked.

I dropped my cooler on the floor and ran to him.

"Camille McPhee," he cheered, tossing me up in the air. On the third toss he sneezed.

"You're covered in cat hair," he said. "Did you buy a cat while I was gone?"

"No," I said.

"Why are you covered in cat hair?" he asked, setting me back down on the kitchen floor. His eyes narrowed with suspicion.

Rather than tell my dad the truth about Checkers/Orca, I decided to tell him something else. Because my parents were in a weird space, it didn't seem fair to rat out my mom to my dad. I was sure he'd be furious with her for giving Checkers away, and I didn't want to make any more waves between them.

"Have you ever heard of Method acting?" I asked. "Lee Strasberg taught it and that's the way we're doing this play. You see, we actually try to become our parts."

Mrs. Zirklezack had spent ten whole minutes telling us about this guy Lee Strasberg. And she'd encouraged us to try to "become our parts" several times.

"So you cover yourselves in cat hair?" he asked, picking several black and white hairs off my pink shirt. "What do the people who are playing crocodiles do?"

His joke worried me. Was he being funny because he knew I was fibbing, or was he just being himself? I couldn't tell. To throw him off, I decided to act emotionally wounded. It was a great trick.

"Do you enjoy mocking fourth graders?" I asked. "Does it make you feel big to tear down our little production?" I flipped my hair over my shoulder and walked away from him.

"I'm not mocking you," he said. "I just—"

"I feel mocked," I interrupted, turning back around to face him. "I know we're not Broadway's best, Dad. But we're trying." Then I crumbled to the floor and began crawling around.

My dad looked very confused. Like he was smelling a certain type of strong cheese, but he didn't know which one and he didn't know why he was smelling it.

"I'm sorry you feel that way," he said, shaking his head. "I didn't realize."

I shot him a hard look and hissed at him. Then I raised my right hand and clawed at the air.

"Camille, I brought you something," he said.

I loved it when my father brought me things.

"Jelly beans?" I asked.

But he shook his head and held out a book. It was about Australia.

"Australia?" I asked.

"It has information about dingoes in it," he said.

"Oh."

It was a big book. I flipped it open to the dingo chapter. There was a picture of a long fence.

"It's to keep the dingoes away from the sheep," my father said. "It's led to an increased number of kangaroos."

"That's horrible," I said. Because I didn't want to think about dingoes eating helpless sheep and interesting kangaroos. "I don't like it when mammals eat other mammals."

"But you eat hamburgers," my dad said.

I frowned. "That's different. We buy them at the store," I said.

My dad smiled. "Do you want to grab something to eat? Would it be okay to eat pizza? Do cats like pizza?" he asked.

"Meow," I said, crawling toward his shoes and rubbing my head against his jeans. For added effect, when he bent down to pet me, I licked his hand. I thought about biting him, but I didn't want to take things too far.

"Let's leave a note for your mom," he said.

Once we got in the car, I dropped the whole cat routine. I explained to my dad that for safety's sake, I abstained from Method acting while in moving vehicles.

"*Abstain* is a pretty impressive word," he said.

"It was a bonus spelling word last week," I said. "My teacher is very advanced."

Eating pizza with my dad was stressful. He wanted to talk about serious stuff. He kept asking about school, and Mom, and my self-esteem, and Mom, and my friends, and Mom, and Mom's self-esteem, and blah blah blah. Then he'd go on and on about his love for me and for Mom and how even if he didn't live at the house, he'd still like to come over and mow the lawn all summer and blah blah blah. Everything always led back to Mom. I wished we'd have been talking on the phone so I could have just pressed the 9 button.

"You're stressing me out!" I finally said. "I don't know what Mom thinks. Hello! I'm Camille McPhee, not Maxine McPhee."

To be honest, when I said this, my mouth was stuffed full of pizza, and no real words came out. I just mumbled in a very angry tone.

"I know, honey. I'm upset too," my father said, rubbing my shoulder and picking off some more cat hairs.

When we got home, my mother wasn't there. She had taped two notes on the kitchen chandelier. One for me. One for my dad. My note said that she wouldn't be home until very late, because she was teaching three aerobics classes in a row. I don't know what my father's note said. After he read it, he folded it up and slipped it in his shirt pocket. Then he faked a very fake smile.

That night, it took me a long time to fall asleep because I kept trying to listen for my mother's car. I planned to eavesdrop on my parents' conversation so I'd know what in the heck was going on. But all I could hear on the other side of my door was silence. Even though I didn't have to use the bathroom, I got up and walked to the bathroom several times. On my last trip, I noticed that my mother still wasn't home. And that my father was stretched out in a sleeping bag on the couch, snoring softly.

When I got up to go to school the next day, my father was outside whacking the weeds. He'd pulled the lawn mower out of the garage too. Which was good. Because Mom had missed several important patches of grass. My father saw me watching him and he waved. I waved back. It was nice having him around again.

When I walked to the refrigerator, I realized that my mom was already gone. I thought it was pretty convenient for her that I hadn't seen her since I'd found out she'd given my cat away. A little too convenient.

My mom and dad had each taped a note for me on the kitchen chandelier. They both wished me good luck on the play, and told me that they'd be there. My father said he'd be there with bells on. My mother said that wild horses couldn't keep her away. Reading those notes, I made an important decision. If my parents ever made it to mediation, I was going to write their mediator a letter and explain how screwed up our ability to communicate was. I may have only been in fourth grade, but I knew that taping notes to a chandelier like this was completely weird. In fact, it was so weird I decided I had to call Aunt Stella.

AUNT STELLA: *Aren't you supposed to be in school?*

ME: *I'm on my way to the bus stop.*

AUNT STELLA: *What's going on?*

ME: *Dad is sleeping on the couch.*

AUNT STELLA: *Sometimes that happens.*

ME: *But sometimes it stops happening, right?*

AUNT STELLA: *Yes, sometimes that's true.*

ME: *My play is today.*

AUNT STELLA: *The one where you're a cat that dies in a rainstorm?*

ME: *Yes.*

AUNT STELLA: *I'm sending you a lot of luck.*

ME: *I think I'll need it.*

AUNT STELLA: *You'll be spectacular.*

ME: *What if I fall off my bucket?*

AUNT STELLA: *You won't.*

ME: *(sigh)*

AUNT STELLA: *I'm going to call you after the play.*

ME: *I think Mom is taking me out to celebrate.*

AUNT STELLA: *Well, I'll call her cell phone. I want to know how things went.*

ME: *She has a new cell phone. Her ringtone sounds like a parakeet and a hammer. But really it's the song of the red-bellied woodpecker.*

AUNT STELLA: *Well, that was always her favorite bird.*

ME: *She buys a lot of things.*

AUNT STELLA: *I know.*

ME: *I wish she didn't. I also wish we didn't have a mortgage. Do you have a mortgage?*

AUNT STELLA: *Yes. Most people who have homes do.*

ME: *That's too bad. Hey, Aunt Stella, Mom's taping notes to the chandelier.*

AUNT STELLA: *For who?*

ME: *Me and Dad.*

AUNT STELLA: *Oh, Camille. Sooner or later, things will improve. They're in a rut.*

ME: *The rut makes me sad.*

AUNT STELLA: *I'm sorry, sweetheart.*

ME: *Me too. I think I better go.*

AUNT STELLA: *Break a leg!*

ME: *That's exactly what I'm worried about.*

I wanted to talk longer, but I knew I couldn't miss the bus. When I looked out my window, I could see Polly shuffling down to the end of my driveway. I wasn't in the mood to see her. I was in the mood to avoid her. Instead of waiting in line, I decided to run out of my house right as the bus was stopping. I downed a banana for extra energy. Then I cracked open my front door and assumed the position that I'd seen runners take in Olympic races.

When the bus brakes gasped, I acted like somebody had shot the starting pistol. You should have seen me fly. I may not have been good at running long distances, but for a fourth grader, I was a very good sprinter.

CHAPTER 31

KNEE-LOCKING

All morning long, I avoided Polly Clausen like she was infected with the superbug. In my mind, I imagined that Polly knew she had the superbug, and that she was purposely trying to track me down so that she could give it to me. But I outsmarted her by peeking around corners before I walked around them.

To be honest, avoiding Polly was pretty easy—she being a parrot, me being a cat. I never really had to look around too many corners, because she was getting ready at the opposite end of the school.

Butterflies zipped through my stomach as the cats prepared to enter the stage for our first performance. All seven of us stood in a line outside the gymnasium. Clearly, I had one of the best tails. It was long and velvet and my mother had sewed it herself with material she had bought several years ago, intending to make throw pillows. Gracie had better ears. She said they were mink, and I believed her, because when I touched them they felt like real fur. Mine were just black construction paper held in place with bobby pins. We all had the same black Lycra bodysuits and tights, although they looked best on Penny, by far the tallest cat. And everyone else had better faces. I couldn't help myself. All morning long—after Mrs. Zirklezack had decorated our skin with face paint—I kept touching my made-up face, smearing my whiskers and rubbing off the tip of my black nose.

I held my big white bucket by its metal handle and stood in my assigned place in line.

You won't fall off, I told myself.

When Mrs. Zirklezack opened the back door, that was the cue for the cats to race into the gymnasium and take their places. When we stood on top of our plastic buckets and sang, "We Can't Go, We Won't Go," Mrs. Zirklezack insisted that we do it with snotty faces and taunting body actions. I wasn't totally sure what a taunting body action was, so I just copied what Penny did.

We were supposed to belt our song right at Nora and her bus of animals as they drove off. We were supposed to sing until the third thunderclap. Then we were supposed to step off of our buckets and curl up and be silent.

I don't know why construction-paper ears made a head itch so much, but mine sure did. With my free hand, I scratched around my ears again and again. I kept knocking them crooked. But Penny was nice. She kept setting her bucket down and straightening them for me.

"You have really nice hair," she said. "It's very silky."

I smiled. And scratched my head again.

"Stop it," Penny said, "or you'll look stupid."

I nodded. I didn't want that.

"I think I'm going to yowl," Penny said, twirling her tail with her hand.

I was surprised to hear Penny say this.

"Mrs. Zirklezack said no noise," Gracie said, flipping around to face Penny.

I liked Penny's idea. I hated that I had to die.

"We should do the play the way we're supposed to," Nina said.

She looked right at me, like she wanted me to support her, but I didn't. I liked Penny's idea better.

"Maybe we could yowl a little," I said.

Zoey Combs didn't like this idea.

"Let's not make a scene. My whole family is coming," she gushed, "even my grandmother from North Dakota. I'm dedicating my performance to her. I've sewn her name into my outfit." Zoey set her bucket down and lifted her long brown hair off her back with both hands. The name THELMA had been stitched onto her Lycra bodysuit. It sparkled across her upper back in little silver sequins.

I thought that was tacky. But maybe I would have felt differently if I had a living grandma.

"I don't know if I'll yowl," Lilly said. "But I might meow a few times. I mean, we are cats."

Penny smiled at me.

Standing in line, I couldn't stop thinking about my mother and my father. I figured they were both already inside the auditorium. They probably wouldn't speak to each other, but it was still nice having them in the same room.

Mrs. Zirklezack opened the back door and waved her arm as if she were directing traffic. "You're on," she said, hitting us on our rears as we rushed past her into the gymnasium. Over a hundred people sat in the bleachers clapping for us. Nora and her bus of animals were almost loaded. She was trying to corral the final pair of chimpanzees.

We stood on our buckets and burst into song, describing how much we wanted to get on the bus. But then, midway through, the song changed its message and we sang about how much fun we were going to have with everyone else gone. We twirled our tails, wiggled our hips, and clawed at the audience with our hands. Mrs. Zirklezack continued to coach us from the sidelines.

"You're sassy cats," she whispered loudly. "Sassy cats!"

I was trying so hard to be sassy that I was sweating like a hog. Which really worried me. Because sweat was slippery stuff.

As our song came to a close, I watched the large cardboard bus close its cardboard door. Nora and the animals inched across the gymnasium floor toward a picture of a sunny mountain. Lots of animals poked their heads out of the bus windows. Even Tony and Boone. I looked down our line at the other cats. This was a bad idea, because it made me wobble. But I was determined not to fall. When things got shaky, I lifted up one foot. I was surprised how easy it was to stand on my bucket on my right leg. Because I was right-armed, right-nostriled, and right-eyed, I figured I was right-legged, too.

I know I was the only cat standing on one leg because I watched the other cats. They did an excellent job clawing at the audience. Except for Gracie. Her legs looked stiff and her body kept swaying.

"I think we've got a knee-locker," I whispered to Nina. "Gracie has locked her knees tight. She's not keeping her pelvis loose like Elvis."

Nina looked concerned. Since first grade we'd been warned by Mr. Fonseca, the choir leader, that when performing we should always keep our knees soft or else they'd lock.

"Bend your knees a little and keep your pelvis loose like Elvis," he'd say, circling his hips wide like a hula dancer.

Mrs. Zirklezack had repeated this several times: "If you lock your knees, you'll faint. And after that, you'll vomit."

I remember being surprised to learn this.

Nina was two cats away from Gracie. Nina was bold. She got down off her bucket and walked over to Gracie. Half of the cats stopped singing. Mrs. Zirklezack was yelling at us to keep going. Cameras flashed in the audience. I couldn't see my mother or my father.

When Gracie went down, she toppled off her bucket like a cut tree. Nina and Penny helped break her fall, lowering her and her stringy hair onto the ground. Which was really nice, because if they hadn't, she could have suffered a contusion. The audience cheered. They thought it was part of the show. Gracie's soft moans were drowned out by the applause. I was the last cat off its bucket, because I wanted everyone to be clear that I hadn't fallen. But in all the excitement, I stepped off my bucket really hard and jammed my big toe. Lightning flickered behind me.

"Ouch!" I said. The pain made me forget where I was. I even forgot I was a cat.

Penny was next to me and she must have thought I had released a yowl, because she started making sounds like she was hurt too, like she was dying.

All of the cats joined in. Even Nina. We cried and shrieked and refused to throw in the towel. It sounded like we were being burned alive instead of slowly drowned. Mrs. Zirklezack had stooped down to our level and was on her hands and knees, slapping the floor from the sidelines and shouting, "No! No! No!"

The lights dimmed as the piano beat out a racket that sounded like thunder.

"I want to live," Penny hollered. "I want to have a family."

"Meow," Nina shrieked.

Lilly, who usually died first in practice, dramatically twitched on the ground.

I looked at the audience. That's when I realized that I didn't want to die either. I would be sending the wrong message to everyone, even my parents. Because life has ups and life has downs. Sometimes you struggle, but I don't think you should ever give up. I think that's true even for cats. So I did what felt right. I did what I thought I'd do if I actually lived in Nora's rainy factory world.

I jumped to my feet and clutched my heart. "Nora," I cried. "There must be room on that bus for one more." I ran to the bus and pulled at the door.

"You're supposed to die," Jasmine Rey snapped at me.

From a small window, I could see Tony Maboney's gray turtle face glaring at me. But I didn't care. I pulled hard on the bus door until it swung open. Mrs. Zirklezack stormed onto the stage and grabbed me by my waist.

"I don't know what this is about," she said, jerking me off the stage. "You're going to damage the props."

The audience laughed. Mrs. Zirklezack pulled me so fast that I couldn't keep up. At one point, she yanked my tail and it came right off. But it didn't hurt. I spotted my mother and father seated in the same row, separated by several people. I blew them kisses.

CHAPTER 32

AFTERMATH

It's hard to find the right words to explain exactly how I felt after being dragged off the stage and having my tail ripped off my butt. But I didn't have much time to think about it. Because I heard my dad's voice. He sounded mad. He sounded like he was blowing up.

My father ran out of the audience and zoomed across the gymnasium's hardwood floor. His thick boot heels left several dark scuffs.

"I can't believe this!" he said. "Stop it!"

He took my tail from me and wagged it at Mrs. Zirklezack. "Get ahold of yourself, lady!" he said.

"This is Mrs. Zirklezack," I said.

"Your daughter is ruining the entire play!" she yelled back. "Look at her."

But he didn't. My father looked Mrs. Zirklezack up and down. "It's life," he said, nostrils flaring. "Fourth graders aren't perfect. Crap happens." His face was bright red.

"Don't use that kind of language with me," Mrs. Zirklezack said.

My father held my tail in his hands and gripped it firmly. When Mrs. Zirklezack had pulled it off, she'd split open an important seam. White stuffing bulged out of the tail's middle.

"You broke her tail," my father said. "Who's going to pay to fix it?"

Then, the next thing I knew, my mother was racing toward us, her hair flying around her face, her high heels clicking across the floor. She sounded angry too. I guess she'd heard what my father had said about my tail, because she said, "We're in public. Stop being such a tightwad!"

My mother grabbed my tail out of my father's hands. "I can patch this," she said.

Because my mother had called my father a tight-wad, I thought he was going to say, "Stop trying to manipulate me, Maxine!" But he didn't. He just stood there.

"Do you want me to go get my bucket?" I asked Mrs. Zirklezack. During practice, we'd been told that it was our job to carry them off the stage.

"I don't want you to set foot on that stage!" Mrs. Zirklezack said. "This is a disaster already."

Lightning and thunder continued to flash and crack.

"This is your fault!" my mother said, pointing to my father.

"No, it's *your* fault!" my father said.

Then my mother let loose a huge list of all the things my father had ever done wrong. He was an emotional firecracker. And a tightwad. And last year he bought her a vacuum cleaner for Mother's Day. And once he dropped a jar of applesauce in the grocery store and walked away and didn't tell anyone. "It's just like you to leave things in a mess!"

And my father had a list of everything my mother had done wrong. She'd bounced more than twenty-three checks since they'd been married. She'd forgotten to bring her passport with her on their honeymoon and they missed their flight to Brazil. She'd driven on a flat tire all day and ruined it. And once she hadn't properly cooked a chicken and they both got food poisoning.

Finally, Mrs. Zirklezack couldn't take it anymore.

"This whole family suffers from an impulse-control disorder." She threw her hands up in the air.

"What's that supposed to mean?" my mother asked. "Camille was only improvising. It's the mark of a true genius."

"Yeah!" my father said.

I guess it was okay for Mrs. Zirklezack to insult them, but not me.

"I said no improvisation!" Mrs. Zirklezack roared. She grimaced at me and revealed her yellow, fanglike teeth. "None! You have betrayed the director and your fellow cast members. Such antics are an offense against the theater!"

I was feeling so light-headed. I felt wobbly and fuzzy and then I tipped over. At first, I thought my father had caught me, but then I felt the gymnasium floor squashing my face. I'm not usually a proud person, but I did feel a little ashamed about tipping over in public right after both of my parents had declared that I was a genius. I wondered if anybody else saw. It wasn't as bad as what had happened with Gracie. She went down in front of everybody. And I was kind of off to the side.

I felt my father scoop me up from the floor. As he carried me out to his truck, I could hear Mrs. Zirklezack insisting that the show must go on.

"For the theater!" she pleaded. Her voice echoed in my ears as I wrapped my arms around my father's neck.

"Did people see me fall down?" I asked.

"Probably not," my father said. "It was dark."

I hoped that was the truth.

"Are you putting her in your car?" my mother asked.

"Yes," he said.

"But I wanted to take Camille out and celebrate," she said.

"She just passed out!" he said.

"But I promised," my mother said.

He released a big, unpleasant sigh.

"Hey, Mom and Dad," I said. "I think I need a piece of cheese."

They both looked down at me as I clicked the seat belt across my lap. Their eyes were filled with softness and worry.

"Where's your cooler?" my father asked.

"Inside," I said. "I couldn't stand on a bucket and hold my cooler and make taunting body actions all at the same time."

"Of course you couldn't," my mother said.

"Should we get it?" my father asked.

"No. It's empty," I said. "I made sure to eat everything before the play."

"I don't have any cheese with me, Camille," my mother said. "We'll have to go to the store."

"One second," my father said. "Your mother and I need to talk about something. Eat this. It has a lot of protein."

My father opened up his glove box and pulled out a piece of beef jerky. He tore it out of its plastic wrapper and handed it to me.

"Mmm. It's salty," I said. "And very chewy."

I watched my mom and dad walk a few feet away. I thought they were going to turn into wolverines again. I kept hoping that one of them would leave, but deep down I knew that a wolverine never retreats. I knew they fought till the end. So right there in the Rocky Mountain Elementary School parking lot, I waited for my parents to attack each other.

I'm not an overly dramatic person, but the next thing that happened was a complete miracle. Instead of hearing the sound of yelling, I heard the sound of a parakeet. And a hammer. Wait. No, I didn't. I heard the song of the red-bellied woodpecker. Then I heard Aunt Stella's voice. I looked out the window. My mother had answered her cell phone and put Aunt Stella on speakerphone. But things got even better! Mrs. Moses walked over and she began talking to my mother and my father and, I guess, Aunt Stella. They were nodding and talking. And nobody was yelling. At one point my mother reached over and rubbed my father's shoulder. Then my father stretched his arm out and hugged my mom. Finally, something fair was happening. They didn't look like wolverines anymore. They looked like my parents! And then I realized something very important. Not only did my parents love me, but they also still loved each other.

I swung open the pickup door and ran to them. But I tripped on a stick and fell right on my face. Dry grass and small pieces of gravel stuck to my smooshed makeup. I must have looked like a very pathetic cat. My parents walked over and helped me up. Mrs. Moses came too.

"Are you okay?" they all asked.

But instead of answering them, I cried out, "It's a miracle!" Then I tipped over again. I fell over another stupid stick.

CHAPTER 33

MEDIATION

After everybody helped me up again, Mrs. Moses asked if she could have a word with me in private. I wasn't thrilled about this, because I was afraid she'd bring up what had happened in the play. I was worried that I might get suspended. I bet this was how the Bratberg kids felt all of the time.

"Camille, life can be challenging." We stood beneath a tree. The breeze blew lightly through our hair. I could see my mother and father waiting for me in the parking lot.

"I agree," I said. "I feel like I'm always being hit with challenges."

"Yes, I bet you do," she said. "I had a talk with your parents. It looks like they'll be attending a seminar."

"That's fantastic!" I yelled. "They've needed mediation for a while. You'd be great."

"No," she interrupted. "It's a financial seminar. Your aunt Stella suggested it, and I encouraged the idea."

"That's perfect. Our Visa bill is huge. We've been in the hole for months!"

Mrs. Moses shook her head.

"Camille, I don't know how things are going to turn out. No one does," she said. "I just want you to know that you can always come and talk to me. I see this a lot." While she spoke, she put her hand on my shoulder and softly squeezed it. "I don't want you to feel like you're in this alone. You're not. And I don't want you to feel like you're in the middle. These are your parents' problems, not yours." The sun was behind Mrs. Moses's head. Her poofy blond hair held its light. She looked like an angel. Except she didn't have any wings. In fact, her arms were very skinny. Her legs too. Mrs. Moses was one of the few people I'd met in my life who I thought should eat more.

Mrs. Moses pulled me closer to her and gave me a hug. Some of my makeup stuck to her pale yellow skirt and I felt a little bit bad about that.

"Don't worry about it. I own spot remover," she said. "By the way, it looks like someone else wants to talk to you."

When I turned around, I saw a very worried-looking, feathery-headed Polly.

"I just wanted to make sure that you were okay," she said.

"Aren't you supposed to be inside?" I asked.

"Once we disembark from the bus, we can pretty much do what we want until we harvest the garden."

"Oh," I said.

"I like what you did. It was nice seeing you stand up for the cats."

"Yeah."

After she said the word *cats,* I could tell that we were both thinking about Checkers. Polly stood there and waited for a little bit. But I didn't say anything else. And she didn't say anything else. It was pretty awkward. Then she turned around and ran back toward the gymnasium. I knew that I should call after her.

Even though I didn't think it could happen, Polly Clausen had become my very good friend. But she had my cat. It wasn't fair. And as bad as I felt about her father dying, I still felt like she should give Checkers back to me. It was a horrible situation. And I didn't want to tell Mrs. Moses about it because I was afraid that she'd make the same suggestion that she gave to me and Penny about the rock and offer to cut Checkers in half for us. I didn't want that to happen, but I had to do something. So I picked up that stupid stick and threw it at Polly.

"Camille," Mrs. Moses said.

"I'm just trying to slow her down," I said, smiling. The stick bounced off Polly's shoe and she stopped.

"I miss Checkers," I said, running up to her.

"I've been thinking about this a lot," Polly said, taking tiny bites of her bottom lip. "My grandma has a time-share in Florida. She gets it part of the time, and other people get it part of the time."

I thought that sending Checkers to live in Florida with Polly's grandma was a lousy idea.

"Maybe we could time-share Orca," she said. "I could have her part of the time and you could have her part of the time."

"I want to call her Checkers," I said. "Orca isn't her name."

"Why don't you call her Checkers," she said, "and I'll call her Orca." She was grinning so wide that I could see her upper gums. Usually this sort of thing would gross me out. But her gums looked healthy and pink and didn't bother me at all.

Looking at Polly and her healthy gums, I wanted to

agree. But I was worried that Checkers might develop a multiple-personality disorder. People on my mom's daytime talk shows were always developing them.

"Okay," I finally said. "That sounds fair." Polly gave me a hug. I turned to run off, but I tripped over another stupid stick! I couldn't believe it. It was like I was living in a land of tripping sticks.

"Shoot," I said. "I can't believe I fell down again."

"Gracie's fall was much worse," Polly said. "She's still in there moaning."

"Yeah, but I wasn't even talking about that one." I stood up and brushed grass off my unitard. (Black is a terrible color to wear if you fall down a lot, because it shows everything.) Then I picked up one of those tripping sticks and I was going to throw it, but instead I just held it. "Sometimes, I feel like there's something really wrong with me."

Polly took the stick out of my hands.

"I don't think anything is really wrong with you," she said.

"But I always fall down," I said.

"And you always get back up. That's what I like about you. You're never on the ground for more than a minute."

Suddenly, I felt a little bit better.

"That's true," I said. "I always get back up. And a

lot of the time, unless I've suffered a contusion, I'm on the ground for a lot less than a minute."

"You're right," Polly said.

I smiled at her. She waved goodbye and I ran toward my parents in the parking lot. I was ready to feel happy. But then I saw my father pop the hood of his pickup. This was bad. Car problems made him blow up.

I frowned. Five minutes earlier, I had experienced a really good miracle. Now, I had to face more problems. Like commercials that I didn't want to see, they just kept coming.

CHAPTER 34

THE AWFUL TRUTH

Luckily, my dad didn't blow up. He'd forgotten to turn his lights off and he'd run down his battery.

"Why don't I drive us all home and we can take care of this tomorrow?" my mother said.

My dad agreed and we all piled into her Chevy. I thought they were already making progress, because they didn't fight over who would drive. Normally, I liked to sit behind my mom, because she left me more legroom. My dad liked to have his seat rolled back pretty far and he reclined it so much that it looked like he was in a dentist chair.

When I got into the backseat, I thought they might think I was picking sides, so I sat exactly in the middle. I dug deep into the seat crack to find the seat-belt buckle. I also discovered a bendy French fry and a raisin. Not a lot of people sat in the middle. And I think the reason not a lot of people sat in the middle was because there was an uncomfortable hump. I decided to endure the hump. Home was only twenty minutes away.

I think that when you're uncomfortable, it's easier to make confessions. Because all of a sudden, for no real reason at all, I started to spill the beans about everything. I told my parents about falling underneath the bus, pretending to be a dingo, calling 911, almost kicking Officer Peacock, sitting underneath the hornet, Tony Maboney poking me, digging up Muffin with Nina, my international calling card, hating Japan, and killing the resurrected fish. I also told them about all the evil things I wanted to do to Tony and I asked them if they knew where to buy fish guts. Then I told them that I'd found Checkers.

"I wasn't going to bring this up, Mom. I was going to try to move on. But I can't. I'm stuck. I loved Checkers. How could you give her away?"

My mother almost swerved off the road.

"I didn't give your cat away," she said. "What are you talking about?"

"Camille, I need to tell you something," my father said. He reached into the backseat and put his hand on my knee. "It was one of the hardest decisions I've ever made. But I knew that we could get you another cat. Polly had become very attached to Checkers, and her father had died so recently. The cat was a special link between them. Life isn't fair, Camille. It's just not, and so I gave Polly your cat."

"You lied to me?" I asked.

I knew that I lied to my father, but I had no idea he lied back.

"And you lied to *me*?" my mother asked.

Then it was sort of quiet. And all three of us just sat there for a minute and thought about what enormous liars we'd been this year. Then my mother broke the silence.

"I can't believe this," she said. "We gave that cat a funeral. We bought two more cats to replace that cat. It's like we're playing God with cats! Talk about bad kismet!"

And even though I should have been very mad, in the spirit of forgiveness and giving everything, including doomed cats, second chances, I decided to let this go. It seemed like the fair thing to do.

"Luckily, Polly and I have worked out a cat time-share," I said.

I could only see the back of their heads, but I was sure that both of my parents were smiling. Then I told them about how Polly and I worked this out on our own, and didn't even need Mrs. Moses's help. I told them about the pink rock and my fear that Mrs. Moses would want to cut Checkers in half.

"That Mrs. Moses is one smart cookie," my mother said.

"Yeah," I said. "I'm aware of that."

"So why do you hate Japan?" asked my father.

Thinking about Sally and Japan and my international calling card with only three minutes left made me so mad I almost kicked the back of my dad's seat.

"It's not good to hate another country," said my mother.

"I hate Japan because Sally moved there and she never wrote me or sent me my kimono."

"Camille," my mother said, "I just got three letters today. She put the wrong zip code on them. They've been in postal limbo."

I didn't know where postal limbo was, but I thought it was rotten that they kept mail that didn't belong to them. My father reached into my mother's purse and handed me the letters. They were in baby blue envelopes and had funny-looking stamps on them. Sally had dotted my name with a heart over the *i* in *Camille*. This made me very happy.

As we drove home, I peeked at one of the letters and saw that Sally had written down her e-mail address. I didn't know she had one of those. I guess her parents changed their rules about computers. This was a thrilling development. I held my letters and took several deep breaths. Reading in cars made me feel like puking. I decided to stop peeking and read the letters when I got home. I didn't think Sally had stuffed a kimono in one of them, but maybe she'd sent me a coupon or something.

It had been a long day.

"Let's pull over here," my mother said, turning into a parking lot by a grocery store we'd never been to before.

"Why?" my father asked.

"They make great pepperoni pizza," my mother said, reaching over and touching his knee.

"Pepperoni pizza," I said, closing my eyes and smiling.

"Look," my father said. "Right next door. There's Dan's Fish Shack. I bet they have fish guts."

I opened my eyes. In front of me, a giant plaster slice of pizza stood on top of a small white building. Next to it, a large green fish attached to a metal pole swam in the air. I tucked my hair back behind my ears and giggled.

"Fish guts," I said.

My mom turned off the car and we opened our doors. The air outside smelled just like a pepperoni pizza. I took a deep breath. That's when I caught a whiff of the fish guts. But that's life. Sometimes you get pizza. Sometimes you get fish guts. Sometimes you get both at the same time. I stepped out of the car and smiled. A cloud moved over the sun, darkening the day. But I didn't care. My mother took one hand and my father took the other. And at last the world felt a little more fair.